W. T. Wallenda

Sniper
at Monte Cassino:
"Sometimes I hear them
still screaming."

from the diary of a
world war II veteran

W. T. Wallenda

Sniper
at Monte Cassino:
"Sometimes I hear them
still screaming."

from the diary of a
world war II veteran

Imprint:

©2024 Wolfgang Wallenda

Cover design, Production and publishing:
BoD - Books on Demand, Norderstedt

Cover pictures:

soldiers-grave-67510_1920

nature-3247227_1280

Pixabay License: https://pixabay.com/de/service/license/

ISBN: 978-3-7578-4522-3

The next war will be more terrible than any of its
predecessors.

Bertha von Suttner
Austrian pacifist
(* 09.06.1843 - † 21.06.1914)

Except for historical personalities, all names have been
changed.

Any similarities with real people would be purely
coincidental.

The Author

Preface

I estimated Josef Altmann to be about 90 years old. Despite his advanced age, he still looked agile and strong. His face was weathered, his gaze friendly. I was very impressed that he had taken the train from Ludwigshafen to the foothills of the Alps just to meet me. Of course, he also had an ulterior motive: he wanted to tell me his life story and persuade me to publish it in book form as another memorial against war.

Mr. Altmann had contacted me through my publishing house. After a few phone calls, I became curious and finally agreed to his request for a personal meeting.

I had already published several books on the Second World War and had met a number of veterans during my previous research. They all told me about their experiences. Not to revive old times, but to save them from oblivion and to warn future generations.

Not a single veteran glorified the Third Reich or the war. They were victims of the times in which they were born, victims of the equalization policies of the criminal Nazi regime, and ultimately victims of the Second World War, which was provoked and started by that regime.

I don't know whether one or two of them became perpetrators during the war. But one thing was clear to me: their experiences, unimaginable for us, were mercilessly etched into the minds and souls of these veterans.

Indelibly!

War is hell.

They told me exactly about this hell.

The majority of ordinary soldiers were drafted involuntarily. Torn from their normal lives, they had to leave their families behind and were condemned to go to war, to fight and kill in order not to be killed themselves. The only human closeness they felt was the comradeship of the man lying next to them in the dirt. The comrade waiting to die with them.

On the fronts of the theaters of war they did not find the much-quoted romance of the Landser or the legendary heroism. They found hardship, misery, suffering and injustice.

They were young and blinded. Infiltrated by nationalist ideas, they answered the call of a dictator and his executioners, partly voluntarily, partly under duress. They went to war in what became the greatest crime in human history.

In their stories, they revealed to me how much this past weighed on the veterans and the invisible burden they had carried with them for decades.

As a result, I now had enough original documents and interviews to write several books. My initial reaction to the telephone conversations with Mr. Altmann was accordingly reserved. But gradually this veteran captivated me. Unlike his former comrades-in-arms, he did not praise my debut novel about Monte Cassino, but told me right away what I had misrepresented in it. It was constructive criticism that I took to heart. Only at the end of his remarks did he say: "You couldn't have known a lot of the little technical details, because it's detailed knowledge from us former members of the Wehrmacht, but one thing is exactly right."

He paused.

"What is that?" I asked curiously.

"The way you described it, that's exactly how it was. Exactly like that. I can judge that. I was there. I experienced it."

After all the justified scolding, this sincere praise was really good.

Two weeks later, I agreed to meet with him. We made an appointment, and after Mr. Altmann arrived, we sat together in the restaurant of the guesthouse where he had rented a room.

After the usual procedure of getting to know each other, he opened a well-worn brown briefcase. His hand went inside and pulled out a stack of papers. He placed them on the table and pushed them toward me. "These are all photocopies. I have the originals at home. Most of them prove my story," he began.

As usual, I prepared a notepad and pen, then leaned back and listened. In a quiet, sonorous voice, Josef Altmann told me about his experiences. After only a few sentences, I was captivated. His narrative style was gripping, unsparing and without pathos. He hardly made a face and only interrupted his flow of words when he took a sip of water or noticed that I was writing over my notes. Only once did the old man become silent in a different way. It was when he was talking about the battles at Monte Cassino. Suddenly he hesitated, then stopped speaking. His eyes became moist, his gaze fixed. He literally looked right through me. It was as if I wasn't even there. At that moment, he was back in his mind. He was in the middle of the battlefields around Monte Cassino, reliving it all.

"Sometimes I can still hear them screaming," he said, his voice cracking.

I got goose bumps.

He closed his eyes for a moment. When he opened them again, the tunnel vision was gone. He had regained his composure, took a sip of water and said: "There were days when young comrades smoked a whole pack of cigarettes or drank a whole bottle of cognac a day just to get through it. It was horrible when the shells whistled and exploded between us. I've never been able to get the images out of my head. It was a battlefield littered with dead and wounded. There were men waving their stumps to get attention. There were young boys crawling out of cover, but they were missing legs. We waded through a mess of blood and bone fragments. And then these shrill screams all the time. You can't imagine, Monte Cassino was hell."

With wet eyes he got up and went to the toilet. When he came back, he sat down and immediately continued his story. I suspected that he was going to get everything off his chest that night. He cleared up everything that was bothering him. After all these decades, he was freeing himself from a heavy burden and wanted to leave it as a warning to posterity.

I promised him that I would use the material someday. He probably already suspected then that he wouldn't live to see it, but he was still grateful to me. As we said goodbye after a long evening, I could see the relief on Mr. Altmann's face. A week later, I received a handwritten letter and his original Africa bracelet as a memento of that conversation. It was his way of thanking me for everything.

Today I'm sitting at my PC, looking at the documents he gave me, opening my notes and keeping my promise.

The Author

Sniper
at Monte Cassino:
"Sometimes I can still hear them screaming"

Africa, mid-March 1943

Between bouts of fever that alternated with chills and blissful heat, I lay awake, at least if you can call that state awake. I was somewhere between reality and delirium. It smelled of urine and feces, carbolic acid, pus, and death. The air was stuffy and hot during the day. At night, however, the freezing cold crept into the unheated rooms and one froze despite two woollen blankets. When there was a rumble at the front, the detonations of the shells could be heard from here. They drowned out the constant moaning of the severely wounded.

A nurse dabbed at my forehead with a damp cloth. A doctor wrote something on a piece of paper and handed it to a medic standing behind him. He mumbled something I didn't understand and then walked away. The look the medic gave me didn't bode well. The nurse tried to pour me some tea. She gently helped me lift my head.

"Just a little sip," I heard her say.

The brown brew was lukewarm. I first moistened my lips and then greedily tried to empty the cup. But as soon as I had taken two small sips, she took the cup away and set it aside.

"You must drink slowly," she warned as she stood up. "I'll be right back."

She walked over to the next hospital bed. Her body instantly became a silhouette. I collapsed again.

It was not my first time in Africa.

I come from a family of artists. My parents owned a small traveling circus that toured Europe from May to October. After more or less successful tours, we returned to the Saarland in late fall. There was our village, which was also our winter home.

We are originally from Alsace. My grandmother was French and my grandfather German. Towards the end of the First World War, in the summer of 1918, they moved to my great-uncle in the Saarland in the German Reich, more by necessity than by choice. We have been German ever since. I grew up bilingual, learning English as a third foreign language on our travels.

Because we were always on the road with the circus, I had never joined the Hitler Youth, which I found very disadvantageous at the time. When we made guest appearances, there were always young boys in Hitler Youth uniforms in the audience. I envied my peers and would have loved to slip into one of those uniforms myself. Especially when we talked before or after the performances and they told me about their adventures in the HJ. The older ones were even allowed to shoot.

I didn't know then that the Nazi regime was training them to become soldiers at a very young age. Both physical and ideological training were on the daily program of the Hitler Youth. The children of today were being molded into the soldiers of tomorrow. One of the slogans of the HJ was: "What are we? Little Boys! What do we want to be? Soldiers!"

My parents were very liberal and avoided talking about politics. My grandfather, on the other hand, raved about Adolf Hitler and his appearance, while my grandmother, understandably, felt more attracted to France and viewed political events in Germany with suspicion.

I was always in the middle and wasn't really interested in politics. It was something else that attracted me. It was the military. Fascinated by uniforms from all over the world and with a thirst for adventure in my belly, I had only one goal: I wanted to be a soldier. Despite my young age, I was already very self-confident and open-minded thanks to my travels and performances in the circus. For me, being a soldier was synonymous with heroism, missions in faraway lands, and pure adventure.

I had been training my body since I was a toddler.

My two older brothers and I swung on trapezes and helped put up and take down the big top. I was way ahead of my biological age, and people always thought I was two or three years older than I really was. I took advantage of this fact during a tour of Alsace-Lorraine in 1938.

I was clearly too young for the Wehrmacht. I didn't see any possibility of being accepted early by forging my papers. I couldn't imagine fooling the German bureaucracy. That's why I kept thinking about enlisting in another military unit. I was attracted to a unit that was already shrouded in legend.

The Légion étrangère.

It was said that everyone was accepted into the Foreign Legion without being asked about their papers. It was the place for adventurers and the gateway to the big wide world. And if you got in trouble with the law, they would give you a new identity. All you had to do was sign up for five years.

Naive as I was, this thought manifested itself in my head, and stubborn as I was, I put my plan into action a short time later.

When we made a guest appearance in Metz, I wandered around the city during the day. I found an advertising office of the Foreign Legion and knew what I had to do. I had made a decision and my mind was made up. After the circus had moved on and the tent had been set up, I packed my few things, left a letter for my family, traveled back to Metz and applied at the office of the Foreign Legion.

I found everything in the Legion, but not what I was looking for. It was a hard and hardscrabble man's world. We were in a fort in the middle of the Moroccan desert and everyday life was dull, boring and dreary. The water smelled of tin, was warm, and always sent one or another of us to the infirmary.

People often lay there with malaria, diarrhea, or if they had contracted a sexually transmitted disease in one of the cheap Arab brothels.

Violence was common among the legionnaires. They drank a lot of alcohol and homosexuality was widespread, probably due to the seclusion of barracks life. Occasionally there were rapes among the legionnaires.

Those who were too weak were disbanded from the legion. Anyone who ended up in a group with the wrong comrades had nothing to laugh about. The physically strong ruled and the weak obeyed, unless they were ice-cold and quick with a knife. Then they were feared.

The military hierarchy was strictly enforced, and discipline was paramount. There were draconian punishments for even the most minor offenses. For example, it was enough to wear unkempt equipment or uniforms, or to sloppily peel potatoes during kitchen duty, to which one was regularly assigned.

Even if they were at odds and hated each other in everyday barracks life, things were different on deployment. Once they marched out of the gate into the desert, everyone stuck together. The troop stood as one man. Everyone gave his life for each other. Nationality or religion did not matter. The German stood next to the Spaniard, the Italian, the Russian and the Swede. The Muslim fought next to the Jew, and the Jew next to the Christian.

Without exception, we adhered to the Foreign Legion's seven-point code of honor.

1. Legionnaire, you are a volunteer who serves France with honor and loyalty.

2. Every Legionnaire is your brother in arms, regardless of nationality, race or religion. You show him your closest solidarity at all times, as if he were your biological brother.

3. You respect your traditions and are loyal to your superiors. Discipline and comradeship are your strengths, courage and loyalty your virtues.

4. You show your status as a foreign legionnaire by your impeccable, always elegant appearance, your behavior is dignified and reserved. Your barracks and quarters are always clean.

5. As an elite soldier, you train tirelessly, you treat your weapon as if it were your most precious personal possession, you constantly strive to improve your physical condition.

6. An order is sacred, you carry it out until it is fulfilled, respecting the law and international conventions - if necessary at the risk of your life.

7. In battle, you act with prudence, coolness, and without hatred, respecting your defeated enemies. You never leave your fallen and wounded comrades or your weapons behind.

When we marched through the desert and sang a song, the inhabitants of the surrounding villages trembled with fear. France showed strength through toughness.

The motto of the legionnaires was then as it is now: Legio Patria Nostra *(The Legion is our Fatherland)* and Honneur et Fidélité *(Honor and Loyalty)*.

I was lucky in two ways. First, I joined a platoon whose hard core consisted of eleven Germans, for whom everyone had respect, and therefore I was never the target of same-sex love attacks. Second, thanks to my good knowledge of foreign languages, I soon found myself in the typing pool, which meant that I only had to take part in a few excursions against rebellious Berbers.

With the outbreak of war between Germany and France, the German and Austrian legionnaires were caught between two stools. For the French, we were half enemies; for the Germans, we were considered traitors to the fatherland, even though we had taken our oath on the flag of the Legion and not on the flag of France. In keeping with our position between two stools, we remained silent and waited to see what would happen.

In 1941, when the German Reich had to help its Italian brothers in arms in Africa, we Legionnaires were remembered. A door to our homeland was opened by offering us the opportunity to join the Wehrmacht.

The motives of the 2,000 or so Legionnaires who accepted the offer were varied. Some wanted to serve their country and fight for the German Reich, while others identified with the regime's nationalist ideas. But most of the comrades I knew, like me, saw it as a quick way to leave the Foreign Legion. It was a way out of the Moloch of the wasteland, where we did our hard service day in and day out for little pay.

Besides myself, nine of my closest comrades volunteered to transfer from the Legion to the Wehrmacht. We went through the usual checks, and when it was clear that there were no wanted criminals or political opponents among us, we were finally integrated into the so-called Reinforced Africa Regiment 361.

However, the reception upon our return to the Reich was not as friendly as we had hoped. We were viewed with suspicion and thrown out of the frying pan into the fire.

Similar to the 500 and 999 probationary units, the 361 Africa Regiment was primarily deployed to the hot spots at the front. We were supposed to rid ourselves of the stigma of being accused of betraying the fatherland. And that's exactly what we did, because we were no ordinary soldiers. We were hard-trained desert warriors who knew the land and the hardships of life in this barren part of the world. We gradually earned respect and recognition, but the price for such a homecoming was high for many Legionnaires. They paid with their lives.

First there was a violent jerk, followed by heavy braking. The centrifugal force made me slide forward. My head hit something hard. I felt a short, sharp pain. I was suddenly awake, but still quite dazed from the fever. I heard the hum of engines. When I opened my eyes I saw a familiar face. It was the round, fiery red moon face of Erwin Mueller from Upper Bavaria, who was always in a good mood. A real good comrade. He's game for anything. It was good to see Erwin. His presence gave me a feeling of security. He was a comrade who never let anyone down, who was absolutely reliable and absolutely discreet. The Upper Bavarian had never betrayed anyone who had done something wrong. Not even when he had been punished himself.

Erwin even served a week in the bunker once, although he had been falsely accused of stealing and drinking a comrade's wine. After Erwin served his week and was released, it wasn't long before a Swiss comrade was in the infirmary with swollen face and broken ribs. The Swiss insisted that he had fallen. But we all knew that Er-win had privately called the real culprit to account.

"Bon jour camarade," the moon-faced man greeted me in French, spoken with his unmistakable Bavarian accent. He laughed. "Well, you old circus clown, have you finally woken up?"

I was on the back of a truck. That explained the jerking and rocking.

"Did you think we were going to leave you behind?"

I tried to answer, but my mouth was dry. My attempt to speak sounded like opening an ammunition box with rusty hinges. Erwin unscrewed the top of a canteen and held it to my chapped, cracked lips. I opened my mouth. He poured some water into it. Some of it ran out of the corner of my mouth and seeped somewhere between my collar and the blanket. What stayed in his mouth was a relief.

"The Tommy is pushing hard against the Mareth line. Our comrades are still holding the line, but it doesn't look good. The military hospital has already been dismantled. It's heading for

Tunis," he said.

I only caught a few words of what Erwin was saying. The fever quickly threw me back into delirium.

The next time I woke up, I saw corrugated iron forged onto twisted steel beams. Propeller engines roared. I was on board a Ju 52, heading for Sicily.

A stopover in a military hospital in Sicily was followed by long stays in military hospitals in Apollonia/Greece and Gars am Inn.

In Apollonia I learned of the fate of the Afrika Korps. The capitulation of my comrades had hit me hard. I didn't know who was still alive, who had been killed, and who had been taken prisoner. What was certain was that the Afrika Korps no longer existed. About 150,000 German and 125,000 Italian comrades had been captured.

When the Allies landed in Salerno, Italy, on September 9, 1943, I was on my way to Gars am Inn. I had lost more than 10 kilos of body weight and was still weak in my legs, but I was on the road to recovery.

In October 1943, I received a field mail letter from my legionnaire comrade Eduard Schwarz. Ede, or Oberlehrer *(Schoolmaste / senior instructor)* as we called him, was quite intelligent. He had the rank of corporal in the Legion. In the meantime, he had been promoted to sergeant in the Wehrmacht. Ede came from a family of lawyers in Cologne and had already studied law for several semesters. Lovesickness had driven him to abandon everything overnight and leave his comfortable life behind. Ede probably found his inner peace in the Legion. The headmaster wrote that Erwin Mueller, Richard Buchecker, Willi Faber and Alfred Kummerer had also escaped from the cauldron. Three comrades from our old platoon were dead, one was missing. All the others were probably captured.

Ede went on to say in his letter that they had been taken to Sardinia. There, the rest of Regiment 361, including about 80 Legionnaires from our battalion, had been incorporated into the newly formed 90th Panzergrenadier Division.

"80 out of the former 850," I muttered, mourning the dead and rejoicing that at least some of my closest comrades had made it. I stared for a few seconds. It was then that I realized that these men were more than comrades to me. They were my friends. The best you could ask for.

In addition to the headmaster and Erwin with the eternally fiery red moon face, three other legionnaires from my platoon had escaped the cauldron.

Alfred Kummerer was from the Palatinate and a trained butcher. He had spoiled us more than once in Africa with delicacies made from freshly slaughtered cattle or sheep.

When I heard the word sheep, I immediately thought of Richard Buchecker. He was a shepherd somewhere on the Baltic coast. Richard was the strongest man I ever knew. I had often suggested to him that after the Legion we could perform together in my parents' circus. He would be presented as the strongest man in the world and would guarantee a sold-out tent. Richard was about six feet tall, and when he stood in the doorway, the room went dark. He had a good disposition. And whoever was considered his friend in the Legion wasn't bothered by anyone. No one really knew why Richard had joined the legion. Richard was extremely taciturn. If he spoke two sentences a day, that was a lot. That's why everyone called him the mute.

Willi Faber was a Street boy from Hamburg. His nickname was Pocke because his face was covered in pockmarks and resembled a cratered landscape. Willi ended up in the Legion because he got mixed up in Hamburg's underworld. "I relieved some pimps of their money while playing cards. I was no longer sure of my life.," he said, grinning mischievously.

A week after I got the letter, I was released as cured. They put me in the Armored Grenadier Replacement Battalion 104 in Landau/Pfalz, and there I was immediately sent on leave, despite or perhaps because of my long illness. I was allowed to go home for 14 days.

But there was no reason to be happy. Grandpa had died two months before. My grandmother told me that Grandpa was proud of me for becoming a soldier. He didn't like the Legion, but he told everyone that I was serving in the Afrika Korps. Unfortunately, there were other bad fates to digest. My two brothers were drafted into the Wehrmacht in quick succession. Both were sent to the Eastern Front. Robert was killed in action at the Dnjepr and was buried somewhere in Russia. Oskar was in a military hospital near Kiev with a bullet in his lung. That was probably one of the reasons I was sent home so unexpectedly.

The time with my family was good for me. They cooked me good food and I visibly recovered. When I went to my unit in Landau at the end of the holidays, I promised my mother that I would write to her from time to time and take good care of myself.

From that day on, I tried to take notes as often as I could.

My time with the Replacement Battalion ended pretty quickly and I had to report to the 3rd Company of the Training Battalion in Neustadt an der Weinstraße.

Only four weeks later I was called back to the office. I was to receive my new transfer. My heart was racing faster than a machine gun. I knew that this time I was going to a front-line unit. Being a former Legionnaire, I had high hopes of rejoining my old gang. I entered the brick building with appropriate excitement, walked quickly down the corridor, and took a few deep breaths in and out in front of the typing pool. The door was ajar and I pushed it open. The spit lifted its head briefly. I smiled, took a step forward and said casually in a polite tone: "Good afternoon. Grenadier Altmann. I've been asked to come here."

A soldier in the typewriter pool skillfully twirled his fingers over the keyboard of a typewriter. Before I had even finished my sentence, the clacking of the levers on the platen immediately ceased. He had stopped typing and was staring alternately at me and then at the spit. The Sergeant Major gave me a sharp, oblique look, turned his attention back to the document he was reading, and signed it.

Sergeant Major in the Wehrmacht was not an independent rank, but a service position. He was the company sergeant and could be recognized by the two spit rings on the sleeves of his field blouse. The „Spieß“ was the *so-called mother of the company*. He relieved the company commander, ran the office, and kept order among the troops in the field. In short, the spit was a person of special respect.

With a grim look on his face, the company sergeant stood up and unexpectedly shouted at me at a tremendous volume: "I think I'm crazy! You will go out immediately, come back and report properly! If you don't, I'll chase you around the barracks yard in full marching gear until midnight! Understood?"

I was stunned and stood there in shock.

"Get out!" He shouted with such intensity that his head turned bright red and the pulsating artery in his neck stood out. His arm shot up like a Hitler salute, only his hand wasn't flat, his index finger pointed at the door. "Out!" he repeated.

I immediately left the office, closed the door behind me, and took a deep breath. I had to digest the scolding for a few seconds. I cursed the commissary, silently cursed the company sergeant, and collected myself. I pushed the door open again and entered the office for the second time. I stamped my boots on the floor without being heard, clicked my heels together, stood at attention and extended my right arm. "Heil Hitler, Sergeant Major. Grenadier Altmann reporting for duty. I've been ordered here."

The Spiess made me wait a minute or two, then leaned back and addressed his assistant. "Schneider, do we have anything on an old man? He can't have been here that long. I don't know the name."

There was a rustle. Seconds later, the soldier in the writing room lifted a document. "He came over from the Fifth. He's a former Legionnaire and is being transferred back to the front." Schneider stood and brought the document to the spit. He glanced at it briefly and beckoned me over to his desk. "Well, there you go. They probably didn't teach you much in the Foreign Legion. We're all about discipline and order here," he said. "Give me the pay book."

I spared myself any comment and handed over the military pay book, only to immediately return to my figure-eight position. The Spike took note and muttered: "Stand at ease."

I pushed my right foot forward slightly.

A few moments later, I pushed my soldier's book back in and held a letter in my hand. It was my marching orders. "As a former member of the 361st Africa Regiment, you are being reassigned to your old unit. Effective immediately, you are assigned to the 90th Armored Division. Regiment, 361st, II Battalion, 7th Company. The marching battalion will leave tomorrow morning at 07:30."

"Yes Sir, Master Sergeant," I replied briskly, suppressing my joy. This was exactly the unit my comrades served in. I would meet the schoolmaster and the others. And if I knew Ede, he had already made arrangements with the sergeant or the company commander for such an event and had my name registered.

"What are you staring at? Did you think we were sending you on Christmas vacation? Get out of here!"

I was satisfied. The whining went in one ear and symbolically slipped out the other.

"Yes Sir, Master Sergeant," I repeated, gave a military salute, turned around and went to my room to pack.

The Wehrmacht was a very modern army with new structures. During its development, it relied on the writings of the French officer Ardant du Picq. Du Picq, who died in the war against Germany in 1870, studied ancient and modern battles and wrote about the fighting ability and morale of soldiers in his book Etudes sur le combat. According to him, men who knew each other fought more tenaciously and stood up for each other, while the cohesion and thus the fighting strength and morale of soldiers who were strangers to each other were not as pronounced. In other words, the closer the soldiers felt to each other, the more stable their appearance as a cohesive unit.

The German Empire took advantage of this situation and built the new army on a patriotic basis. Men from the same regions served in the same units. They spoke the same dialect, had the same attitudes, and often had known each other for years or were even related. It was not until casualties increased as the war progressed that this type of recruitment could no longer be targeted.

The next pillar of the Wehrmacht's military success was training. Every German soldier was so familiar with his weapon that he could take it apart and put it back together blindfolded. This meant that they did not panic, or at least panicked less, when their rifles jammed, as the problem could often be solved in a few simple steps.

Another positive innovation was a small but effective

change to the internal structure. During the First World War from 1914 to 1918, there had been a strict separation between enlisted men, NCOs (Non-Commissioned Officers), officers and general staff, but in the Wehrmacht things were different.

If qualified, every soldier had the opportunity to rise to the top.

Every member of the Wehrmacht, from the common soldier to the field marshal, received the same food.

Orders were discussed in detail. When you went into the field, even the common soldier knew what the order was and what the objective was. If the officers fell, the NCOs led; if they fell, the next rank led. The men could act and were not helpless if a superior officer fell.

December 21st, 1943

We marched out of the barracks with the *Westerwald song* on our lips. We radiated a cheerful serenity to the outside world. The young recruits, the majority of the men, were beaming with pride and joy. They dreamed of heroism and me-dals. The older ones among us, mostly returnees from military hospitals or units that had been wiped out, were more reserved. They knew the war, the front, the hardships and the hell on earth that came with it. They knew what to expect.

I myself had mixed feelings. On the one hand, I was looking forward to seeing my comrades again, but on the other hand, I was afraid that I would have to go into battle again. Killing was cruel. Lying behind a machine gun and firing into a swirling mass coming at you was less touching than meeting the enemy on a reconnaissance patrol and killing him with a bayonet, a spade, a dagger, or your bare hands to save your own bare life. I had to learn this bitter fate of the soldier in Africa. Kill or die. I wanted to live, so I inevitably killed. The night patrols in the already inhospitable desert were feared and hated. You almost always met the Tommy, and that meant hand-to-hand combat.

I closed my eyes as these memories flashed through my mind. How many sleepless nights had I spent because of this? How often had I been haunted by the faces of the men I had to kill? They danced around me like devil's grimaces until I woke up in a cold sweat. It got better with time. But it never stopped.

To distract myself, I joined in the singing and belted out the next verse at the top of my voice. "... the wind whistles so cold over your heights, but the slightest sunshine penetrates deep into your heart ..."

We all didn't know that we were marching straight into a hell of unimaginable proportions. The devil pushed the gate to his realm wide open. The entrance gate was called Monte Cassino. Thousands and thousands of soldiers were to pass through it. And we marched towards it in high spirits and singing loudly.

It was a good thing that none of the men had the slightest idea at that moment that around three-quarters of them would be dead within the next six months, were considered missing in action or would be languishing in a military hospital, some of them seriously wounded.

The sergeant leading us seemed to like the song very much. As soon as it was over, he shouted loudly: "And one more time! Let's go, comrades!"

And so it resounded again at the top of its voice: "Today we want to march, try a new march, to the beautiful Westerwald, where the wind whistles so cold ..."

We had to cover around 1200 kilometers to get to the front. On foot, by truck and mainly by train.

Six long days had passed since then. On Christmas Eve, we were accommodated in a hotel, but there were only enough rooms for a few of us. Most of the group slept on camp beds in the large reception hall or in the dining room. Beforehand, we celebrated Christmas together. We had a thin broth as a starter, then a very good roast with dumplings and red cabbage, and for dessert we were served chocolate pudding. The atmosphere changed from a friendly, cozy atmosphere to quiet contemplation. Those were the minutes, sometimes hours, when everyone was lost in thought about home and family. There were only a few of us who sat together in a corner until well after midnight, playing cards and laughing.

One day later we spent the night in a barracks and on the following two days and nights we stayed in the wagons of the troop transport. Fresh straw served as bedding and a cannon stove, stoked with wood and some coal, provided pleasant warmth.

When we left Germany for the Alps in sleet and snow, it was only two degrees plus and it was cloudy and gray. In southern Italy, we hoped for better weather. We talked about what it would be like there and agreed that we had drawn the middle lot of the three big fronts with Italy. France would have been better and the loser was, of course, the Eastern Front. Nobody wanted to go there. So we were all happy. We had all ignored the fact that you could die in agony on any of these fronts.

I had a seat near the stove and found the train journey relatively pleasant.

The superiority of the enemy air force was clearly noticeable in the approach of the troop transports, among other things. To avoid being a target for the Allied fighter-bombers, we mainly drove in the dark.

We quickly became accustomed to the *ch-ch-ch of* the locomotive and the clacking as it passed over the sleepers. The atmosphere in the carriage was quiet and restrained at first, later cheerful, almost exuberant. We passed the time playing cards and having lively conversations.

One of the Landser played the harmonica really well and spread additional cheerfulness. At one point, however, the comrade also provided a melancholy calm. We were on a train somewhere near Merano. We had been sent out to stretch our legs while the locomotive was supplied with coal and water. When we came back, the harmonica player was already there. He had put a few logs on the fire and then sat down on his straw bed. Without looking at us, the soldier pulled out his harmonica and began to play *Heimat deine Sterne*. A hit by Wilhelm Stienz. It was a cold, starry night. Four or five comrades sat in the wagon, a few stood in front of it and listened to the melody. Some were humming along. Others, who knew the words, joined in with the singing. When the song was over, no one spoke. An oppressive silence. Sad songs by Lale Andersen and Zarah Leander followed.

The man next to me fought back tears. The comrade in front of me took a photo of his family from his breast pocket and cried quietly. Only the whistle of the locomotive interrupted the contemplative musical interlude. A couple of sergeants called for passengers to board. The small crowd in front of our car dispersed. A moment later, one of the men pulled the heavy door at the entrance shut. The locomotive jerked to a stop and rolled out into the cold, dark night.

We were inexorably approaching our destination, which was near the metropolis of Rome. By the time we arrived at the station, we had gotten to know each other so well that it was almost difficult to say goodbye. Hands were shaken and some men arranged to meet for a beer, if the situation at the front allowed it.

The first orders rang out across the compound. Soldiers rushed around and we left the car. It was like an anthill.

"You see, it's not much warmer here than at home. It's only 12 degrees," I said to Elmar Roeder, who also belonged to II/7.

I had just met Elmar on the train. He was 19 years old and

a trained baker. Although I was hardly older, I looked much more mature. I had the feeling that the African sun had not only tanned my face, but also taken years off it.

Field gendarmes *(Military Police)* scurried around in several small groups, checking the marching orders of their comrades again and again. If someone didn't know what to do, they pointed to the many signs that were posted almost everywhere. I looked around and read "Field Hospital," "Assembly Point," or "Command" on the signs, and then made my way to the assembly point. Elmar followed me. A group of young soldiers marched up behind us, led by an older corporal. They quickly caught up and the corporal joined me. He introduced himself as Heinz Krueger and was one of the soldiers returning from leave.

Within a short time so many men had gathered around us that we had almost reached the strength of a company. In front of the assembly point a sergeant finally ordered us to line up properly, and half an hour later we were sitting on trucks that were to take us to our units.

Krueger was also with the 7th Company. He told us that our group had been fighting near Ortona until a few days ago and had suffered heavy casualties. Krueger didn't say where he got this information. He probably knew one of the field generals who had told him.

The lance corporal was the perfect example of an organizer. He always had an easy line, knew God and the world, and when he went out to make a kill, he came back with his pockets full to bursting. He had shown this organizational talent in Meran. During the stopover, he had set out with the words: "Wait for me, I'll have a look around. Maybe I can get some special provisions for the trip."

Krueger returned only a few minutes before the train left. I was already thinking about how to explain his absence and was relieved to see him running to the platform. Slightly out of breath, he put down his backpack. "I had to walk a little farther," he gasped, unpacking his haul. He presented six bottles of wine and a large ham wrapped in paper. When asked about the origin, the corporal just grinned. "If you ever need anything, ask old Krueger. I can definitely help you."

The wine and ham were then shared in good company, and the unexpected delicacies created a good atmosphere in the wagon.

As we walked the last stretch to the company, I had become very quiet and thoughtful. I spoke very little, and when I was asked a question, I answered in short, concise sentences. I don't know if this was passed on to the other soldiers. In any case, the general atmosphere was completely different from that on the train. With every kilometer we got closer to the front, everyone seemed to be more and more lost in thought.

The countryside was hilly and barren. To the south were the Alban Hills, to the east the Abruzzi, whose foothills were not visible. The terrain was a reflection of the weather: extremely rough.

We passed through several small villages. The locals hardly looked at us. And when they did, they were anything but friendly. In my opinion, the resentment of the Italian population was completely justified. Since the fall of Mussolini, we Germans were no longer their allies, but enemies occupying their country. Germany had gone from being Italy's closest brother in arms to its enemy. Moreover, the Allies were getting closer and closer, and that meant war. War meant death, destruction, suffering and flight. And that's why they hated us. We were a magnet for evil and brought war right to their doorsteps.

Every now and then a child would wave to our little column. Roeder always returned the greeting, and once he even threw a few drops at two girls. They ran away laughing. We could no longer see them picking up the candy. The driver of our truck had turned off and was driving the Opel Blitz over a hill. The road was barely paved. If it hadn't been cold and wet, we would certainly have dragged a cloud of dust behind us, visible for miles. We could hear the gears shifting, the driver shifting between them with a crash. The engine roared as it struggled with the incline. The roads were in very bad shape and full of potholes. We were constantly pushed up and down on the wooden benches. Once we reached the top of the hill and started rolling downhill, the truck quickly picked up speed. Inevitably, we bumped through a deep pothole and were literally thrown up, only to land roughly on the hard bed again. This time, however, so hard that I feared a tire had burst. In my mind's eye I saw us changing the tire, but the Opel Blitz continued on without a hitch.

Lucky me, I thought.

"What a terrible driver," grumbled Krueger, who had squinted his eyes at the painful impact. "My whole ass is guaranteed to be a single bruise."

With this statement and the corresponding facial expressions, the *old warhorse* had once again managed to break the oppressive mood and make us laugh. The men visibly relaxed. The first conversations began.

"Heinz, wouldn't you have preferred to spend Christmas at home with your family?" Elmar Roeder wanted to know from Krueger.

The lance corporal grimaced and shook his head wildly. "No, never! Boy, I have more problems at home than at the front. My wife gave birth to a sixth child in November. That's why I got leave. But my mother-in-law has moved in with us. No one told me about this beforehand. Under these circumstances, I decided to shorten my vacation and celebrate Christmas with you. I thought, instead of looking at my mother-in-law's unshaven face every day, I'd rather look at the kitchen bull's face when he fills my dishes. And let's face it, guys, the food in this hotel wasn't that bad.

Everyone laughed again.

When the convoy stopped half an hour later, my heart was pounding. We were there. Questions raced through my mind.

Which of my comrades were still alive? Who would I meet again? How had they fared in Ortona?

Heinz Krueger jumped off the truck and cursed loudly. "Damn, I'm glad to be here. Another three kilometers and I wouldn't have been able to sit down for a week."

One by one we got off the truck and looked around.

The village where the company had been billeted was nestled between the foothills of the mountains. The nearest larger village was several miles away and difficult to reach. We were pretty much cut off from the outside world here. At least that's how those of us who lived in a town at home felt.

Some of the houses were whitewashed, but most were unplastered and stone gray. There was no sign of a bustling Rome here.

The quartermaster had soldiers in almost every building. We also occupied the town hall and the small school with its two classrooms. The company vehicles were mostly hidden under camouflage nets or covered with straw or greenery to avoid being spotted by enemy reconnaissance aircraft.

The locals were reserved with us. I had the feeling they were really hiding. Only a few old people and small children could be seen from time to time. The young men and women had probably left the village in fear of us Germans and had sought refuge with relatives.

Friends had become enemies, I thought. Even if some of my comrades didn't understand this behavior, I could understand the attitude of the Italians after thinking about it for a while.

A deep, raspy voice thundered toward us: "Fall in!"

It sounded as if the guy had put a rubbing iron behind his larynx. I couldn't see the caller and imagined a big, burly man. One thing was clear from that one word: This soldier was used to giving orders.

Krueger's head flew around. "Crap," he muttered softly.

"That's the spit. Come on, comrades. Sergeant Major Klemm eats small children for breakfast. Now it's time to parry."

We immediately followed Krueger and lined up according to size. When the sergeant major came over to us, I was amazed. Klemm was not much taller than 1.60 meters. His head was almost shaved. Only the outline of his hair was visible. He looked wiry. I guessed he was incredibly tough on cross-country marches. His uniform fit perfectly and his boots shone. With a familiar wave of his hand, the bald man disappeared under a cap. He stopped in front of us. He looked at us intently.

Krueger stepped forward as the highest ranking officer, saluted and reported. "Corporal Krueger reports from leave, Master Sergeant. I've brought 14 new comrades with me."

"Krueger," it shot out of the spike's mouth. "Why the hell are you back already? I know you're not the brightest star in the firmament, but even you can remember an appointment."

Some of the soldiers laughed. Klemm's eyes immediately darkened. "Silence in the corridor!"

A jolt went through the line. In an instant, all noise was silenced. Klemm turned back to Krueger. "Tell me in one sentence why I have to look at your face and how you managed to come back to the front despite being on leave? I didn't expect you back before Epiphany."

The corporal grinned. "I had the choice between your command and my mother-in-law's, Sergeant Major. Guess which one is worse."

Not even the company sergeant had expected this reaction. His intended scolding withered. He visibly fought not to laugh out loud. The corners of his mouth pulled back far and were pulled back again almost violently. This was repeated a few times before he had fully regained his composure and control. "Back in the limb."

Krueger quickly got back in line.

The Spiess walked down the line. "Welcome to the 7th

Company. There is discipline and order here. Orders are followed and dissent is not tolerated. The clerk's office is in the town hall of this miserable nest. You will now march there under the command of Lance Corporal Krueger and enter one by one. Show your marching orders and pay books without being asked. We will then tell you which platoon to report to and where to find it.

A short pause followed.

"Your comrades are on a field exercise," he continued. "If you think you're soldiers, you're wrong. What you've been taught so far is like an empty backpack. We still have a lot to teach you, and we will fill that backpack. Only then will you become real soldiers. Our new division commander, Major General Baade, places great importance on good training. I will fulfill his wish."

When he reached the end of the line, he turned around, walked to the center of the group, and stood with his legs apart in front of us. "And now again in my own words. If you think barracks life and basic training are hard, you're wrong. This is where it all starts. We make you real soldiers. If you're too weak, you'll break. If you don't parry, you'll be put on special duty. Any questions?"

Silence.

"Which of you rug rats has served?"

Krueger stepped forward. "Me, of course, Sergeant Major!"

The spit swallowed. His Adam's apple moved up and down. His cheeks and forehead flushed.

It was immediately clear to me that he didn't find Krueger's humorous interlude particularly funny this time. To ease the situation a little and to distract Krueger's attention, I also stepped forward. "I, Sergeant Major. I served in the Foreign Legion and then fought in Africa with Regiment 361."

Done. The spearhead literally flew around. The small brown eyes seemed to pierce me. "Another legionnaire," he hissed.

I stood at attention and answered briskly. "Yes Sir, Master

Sergeant."

"Name?"

"Private Josef Altmann, Master Sergeant."

The spit came closer. He looked at me, my uniform and my luggage with a critical eye. At that moment, I wondered if all Wehrmacht spies were the same and if they had a course in unsympathetic and violent behavior. They also used almost the same words to silence us.

They have a spear guide, I thought.

I was expecting anything but what happened. The sergeant major stepped back, took a last look at me and said: "Thank you, stand at ease."

I relaxed my posture and pushed my right leg forward slightly.

Klemm had turned to the other men. "Soldiers! This comrade fought for us in the desert. I know what the legionnaires did in Africa. We stood side by side against the Tommy. They made up for their mistake of fighting for another army. Stay with him, and you will learn to march, to obey, and to fight. All in all, you will learn to survive." He was silent for a few seconds and then added, "I'll see you in the writing room in five minutes. I'm handing over command to Corporal Krueger. Thank you, dismissed."

After the bureaucracy was over, I waited with the other comrades in front of the town hall until everyone was ready. Then one of the two soldiers from the office led us to our respective accommodations. He was limping a little on his right leg and was quite talkative. He told us more about the fighting around Ortona and confirmed the rumors that there had been heavy casualties. According to him, the troops there had only been deployed in battalions and had been gradually worn down. Our company had been hit very hard and a number of former Legionnaires had fallen in the fighting.

"And in the end, it cost the commander his head," he said.

"The new one, Major General Baade, is completely different. He turned the tide and some of the incompetent officers..." he cleared his throat and looked around to make sure the wrong person wasn't overhearing, "... so he literally sent them into the desert. Stripped them of their command for incompetence."

Krueger walked beside me. He suddenly lifted his nose and sniffed. "What's that smell in the air?"

The private stopped and pointed to a large barn with the door wide open. Clouds of steam poured out. "General Baade has also seen to it that the cooks always have something decent in the cauldron. He believes that the field kitchen is like a magnet. Wherever it is, so are the Landser. So they are always way ahead. And the better the food, he says, the better the mood of the soldiers. Our field kitchen is in that barn over there.

Krueger rubbed his stomach with one hand. "I like this new old man," he grinned and added, "Smells like strong goulash."

"Major General Baade also attaches great importance to good training. That's why we spend six days practicing, practicing, practicing, and on the seventh day the equipment is spruced up."

Krueger grimaced at this comment. "I don't like that at all. I could almost sense that there was a catch somewhere. It sounded too good to be true."

The private stopped in front of the village schoolhouse. "Krueger, Altmann, Roeder, Gebhardt, Thaler and Wimmer. You belong to Sergeant Schwarz's group. Your entire group is quartered in the schoolhouse. Straw beds have been provided."

Fate had been kind to me. I was very happy to be reunited with my good comrades from the Legion. I was also glad that Heinz Krueger and Elmar Roeder were also in the Schwarz group. We had become good friends during the trip and I liked them.

After refreshing with us, our group had reached the original standard strength of 1/9.

I also liked the fact that our group was all in one building, while the other two groups in our pla-toon were split up into several houses. Personally, I would have felt uncomfortable being forced to stay with complete strangers, possibly against my will.

Although the soldiers always befriended the forced laborers, there were often hostile glances. I just felt safer when we were alone. There was one thing you could never forget: We were the foreigners in this country. We were the intruders, and we were the ones who brought the war here and tore the local families apart. We were the ones who took the last of their livestock or part of their crops to feed ourselves. And we were the ones who hunted down and killed their sons, fathers, brothers or friends when they joined the partisan gangs to fight against the injustice we had brought with us.

To call it a school building flattered the old house. There were two classrooms, large enough to accommodate only four or five men with their equipment. Ede had made himself comfortable in the third room, which was only half the size of the other two. It must have been the village teacher's living room. The wooden benches for the students had been placed in the courtyard by their comrades. The building was heated by a stove in the hallway of the house. There was firewood next to it.

I chose the room where there was one free and four occupied straw beds. I noticed that my fellow legionnaires had taken up residence here. Meanwhile, Krueger and the four other Landser had made themselves comfortable in the spare room.

We had just stowed away our luggage and spread the canvas and blankets over the straw when our comrades returned from the field exercise. I looked out the window and beamed with joy. There they were. My legionnaires. I quickly ran to my pack and took out the two bottles of plum brandy I had brought with me. As soon as I had them in my hand, I stared into the astonished, red-cheeked face of Erwin Mueller.

"Bon jour, camarade," I greeted him.

"Bon jour, Sepp," came back, although Erwin's bon jour

sounded, as always, unmistakably Bavarian. It sounded like he was saying poar Schuah, which means a pair of shoes, in his Bavarian dialect. Erwin was the only person who called me by my nickname, Sepp. He insisted on the Bavarian short form of my first name. Every other one of my comrades called me Jupp or Josef. "You look like a gnawed bone. Didn't they give you anything to eat in the hospital?"

Erwin grinned broadly when he saw the bottles of schnapps in my hands.

One by one, the other comrades pushed their way into the small room. Shoulders were patted, hands shook. The plum brandy was passed around. Everyone took a big swig. "Good stuff. Home-distilled?"

"How can you ask such a stupid question?" commented Erwin. "If the schnapps is in wine bottles, of course it was distilled by yourself."

Ede Schwarz was the last of the group to enter. "Jupp, old warhorse," he called to me. "I'm glad to see you again. I had my doubts if you'd come back at all."

The schoolmaster looked more mature and somehow more used up than I remembered him. The NCO stripes looked good on him. "Weeds don't die," I waved him off, pointing at his epaulettes. "They look good on you."

Ede saw the bottles of booze floating around. "No more drinking, men. We welcome the newcomers, then we clean our equipment. Roll call is in an hour. If our platoon leader, Lieutenant Kohler, smells a flag, there'll be a big scolding, and if the company commander, Captain Geller, smells a flag, there'll be punishment."

Grumbling, the bottles were sealed. Ede had the whole group line up in two rows, old and new comrades facing each other. The introductions began. Weapon and equipment maintenance followed. While cleaning the weapons, I learned firsthand about the battalion's battles and how positively the guiding hand of the new division commander was felt.

Ede told us about our new area of operations: the Gustav Line. This gigantic defensive line was located about 100 to 150 kilometers south of Rome. "The positions begin at the mouth of the Garigliano River and extend over Monte Cassino to the headwaters of the Rapido River and on over the ridge of the Apennines to the Adriatic Sea. Right across Italy, so to speak. And so we block the Via Casilina with the core section of Cassino. This is the only road on the west coast of Italy from the south to Rome where tanks can get through. There is no other route for heavy vehicles in the entire southwestern boot of Italy. Whoever controls the road and the mountain controls southern Italy and therefore Rome. And from Monte Cas-sino you can see the whole plain. That means a wide view and the best field of fire."

The mute tapped me on the shoulder and pointed to my rifle. It was clean as a whistle. He raised his thumb and nodded approvingly. Moonface Miller was hungry. "The field training is annoying. I only get a few slices of bread at noon, and my stomach growls until dinner. I'd like to know which idiot ordered us to eat something hot in the evening instead of lunch.

"Psst," breathed Willy Faber. Pocke had put his index finger to his lips. "Not too loud. Captain Geller is creeping through the village. He'll have the company line up later to welcome the new recruits in person."

General groans and eye rolling. None of the men wanted a visit from the boss.

"How do you know that again?" Erwin wanted to know.

Pocke shrugged. "I just know."

It turned out just as our Hamburg boy had predicted. Geller showed up, introduced himself again, gave a rousing speech, and told us that although we had lost Africa, Fortress Europe was impregnable. Then he raved about the new division commander, Major General Baade, and sang his praises about his ideas on soldiering: He was pushing the training of the troops and emphasizing basic discipline. The duty roster consists of many exercises so that what is learned can be put into practice in combat.

In accordance with our company commander's conviction, the next two weeks were spent in almost barracks-like drills. This time was characterized by field and marching exercises of all kinds.

Ede was not squeamish with us, but he didn't exclude himself either. The company commander was also often in the field. Captain Geller turned out to be a full-blooded officer and an avowed National Socialist. In his presence we neither made jokes nor allowed ourselves any mischief.

Our platoon leader, Lieutenant Kohler, on the other hand, was a different sort of man. He was also concerned with uniform and discipline, but unlike Geller, he was polite and always sat with us during breaks in the field. He instilled an absolute sense of togetherness. After ten days, he organized a small dinner for the platoon, where there was plenty of red wine and sutler goods. We had prepared the largest room in the so-called town hall of the village. We sat there in close quarters. At a late hour and after a few glasses of wine, Kohler told us that Geller was suffering from a sore throat. He longed for medals. "Our boss wants to get the Knight's Cross by force. His father was a bigwig on the general's staff in the last war and had dozens of medals pinned to his chest. Geller's brother is a colonel somewhere in Russia and has already been awarded the Knight's Cross," he said.

We were not very enthusiastic about our company commander's thirst for medals, especially since we had seen a similar example of medal addiction in Africa. Back then, it was our platoon leader who had volunteered for every mission in order to finally get his Knight's Cross. We had him to thank for the fact that we went on four out of five scheduled patrols a week. He didn't survive the last one. A Tommy had cracked his skull open in hand-to-hand combat.

The newcomers fit in well with the group and I quickly felt like a soldier again. After the first two off-road exercises, I was physically exhausted, but then it went uphill and I was able to handle the effort better and better. My stamina returned. Maintaining my equipment, on the other hand, was no problem. Cleaning my uniform and weapons had become second nature to me since my days as a recruit in the Legion.

I also excelled at marksmanship and was in a constant duel with Ede for first place. I was actually ahead of him most of the time.

Little did we know at the time that the mixture of veteran Wehrmacht soldiers, former Foreign Legionnaires and young recruits, who learned a lot from us in a very short time, would result in a strong fighting force.

This in turn meant that, as in Africa, we would be deployed at the focal points of the front.

The 90th Panzergrenadier Division quickly became an elite unit.

January 19, 1944

In the middle of the night, the UvD *(Sergeant on duty)* ran through the village and woke us up. "Alarm! Everybody out! Get up! Assemble at the town hall!" he shouted into the hallway, turning and running to the nearest shelter.

"Ouch! Damn," thundered from the other room. Kruger had stubbed his toe in the dark.

"What's going on?" came sleepily from a corner of my room.

Cursing, coughing, rumbling. Finally someone turned on the light. I shivered and immediately slipped into my socks and pants, pulled on my sweater, and put on my boots.

"Get out of bed, men! Get dressed and take your guns with you," yelled Ede Black.

"What's going on?" was asked again.

"You heard the headmaster. The alarm. We have to line up."

Krueger ranted. "If this is another one of the old man's drill pranks, I'll pee in his coffee myself."

"This is no drill, Heinz. Panic was in the UvD's voice. Something wild is rolling towards us."

Minutes later, we were standing in front of the town hall and for-med up. The lights in the building were on. We could see the hustle and bustle through the uncurtained windows. The radio operators were housed next to the company sergeant's room. They were sitting in front of their radios, taking down one transmission after another. Captain Geller stood in the sergeant's office, holding the bakelite receiver of the field telephone to his ear. His gestures were frantic.

A haze of breath hovered in front of our mouths. "What time is it?" I asked Pocke, who stood beside me and yawned.

"A little after three," Ede whispered before I could answer.

I saw our captain hang up the phone and give some instructions to the Spit. Shortly after, they both left the building.

"Attention!" commanded Klemm and a jolt went through the company.

Before the Spittoon barked any more orders, the company commander stepped into the middle of the platoons lined up in a square. "At ease," he said in an unusually casual manner, and we took our places.

"Since yesterday, the Allies have been pressing against the Gustav Line with massive forces on a broad front. The French, Americans and British are advancing simultaneously. In the Garigliano estuary, our comrades of the 94th were pushed out of their positions by British troops. Minturno was lost and the enemy crossed the river with their first tanks. The British were able to penetrate deep into our defensive bulwark. We were ordered to go to Priverno and then to intervene on the Garigliano front. Departure in 30 minutes. Coffee, tea and cold rations are distributed. Platoon leaders to me. Dismissed!"

Just before the scheduled departure, Lieutenant Kohler came to us. He announced that three battalions and an engineer company from our division would form the reserve for the defense of the coast near Rome. We also learned that the division had been inadequately replenished and, despite replacements, was barely three-quarters of its combat strength. Our group was one of the companies that was still in a fairly good position in terms of manpower and was therefore part of a battle group. More troops, equipment and ammunition were to follow by rail.

The first problems arose during the loading of the trucks. There was a shortage of fuel. Captain Geller went on a rampage, rounding up everyone he could find. The phones were ringing off the hook and trucks from both the supply train and the combat train were rolling out to get fuel. A group of Grenadiers went along as escort.

After a delay of four hours, which at least gave us some sleep, we also left.

The convoy moved slowly. Trucks kept stopping to wait for more fuel. There were also regular air raid alarms and we had to take cover a few times. There was hardly any talking. My comrades and I were mostly lost in thought or dozing. Only Krueger slept soundly. He snored softly to himself, and when he let out a deep grunt, he woke up, opened his eyes briefly, mumbled something unintelligible, and then went back to sleep.

A number of civilians, who had fled their homes in fear of the approaching front and were streaming north, came towards us.

"Poor bastards. They have to leave their homes, and when they come back, it's all rubble and ashes," said Erwin Mueller. He was our machine gunner and held the weapon between his legs. A belt drum was attached and a belt of ammunition hung around his shoulders.

He had been assigned two of the newcomers as shooters number two and three. They were Thaler and Wimmer. They sat next to Erwin on the wooden bench.

The louder the rumble of the guns, the quieter the conversation.

"You can talk loud," laughed our moon face as Wimmer began to whisper. "The Tommys can't hear us."

The Allies were firing from two directions. Their artillery positions behind Minturno attacked the front line and the warships of the Allied fleet bombarded the battle area from the sea.

Priverno was in turmoil. If it hadn't been for the gendarmes, we would have been mercilessly caught up in the confusion of refugees, ambulances, supplies and our advancing regiment.

We stayed in the village just long enough to smoke a cigarette or walk to the exit. After a few minutes, Lieutenant Kohler ordered us to report. He told us that we had to move on to Itri immediately because the battalion was part of a combat group there and the attack was already underway. I was surprised because at first we were told that our attacks would be supported by the air force, but I hadn't seen any of our planes yet.

We looked at each other questioningly. According to our platoon leader, we should have been in our launch positions long ago. The chaos was enormous. There were murmurs. Lieutenant Kohler became louder: "Men, the 94th was completely untested in combat. It was badly banged up. The Tommy is pushing with all his might and has already extended his bridgehead far beyond the Garigliano. We have to push him back, and for that purpose we, as well as units of the Herman Göring Panzer Division, are subordinate to the 94th.

The drivers grumbled at first, then began to grumble loudly. "We can't go another three kilometers. We need fuel! The tanks are empty."

Kohler was furious and immediately sent his driver back to the radio operators to solve the fuel problem. They were told to apply pressure through the battalion with an explicit situation report, which they did. Half an hour later an Opel Blitz arrived with dozens of fuel cans on the back. We all helped to unload, and when our trucks were full, we got in and drove the last stretch to the HKL *(Hauptkampflinie = Main battle line)*.

We knew we were going into battle. To reassure ourselves, we told ourselves that the rumbling and thundering was not only coming from the enemy, but that our artillery was also firing and keeping the enemy at bay. That calmed us down a bit.

"Boys, when we leave later, make sure you have your canvas tents and packs with you. It'll be dark soon, and if they throw us into battle now, we won't be able to disengage so quickly," Corporal Krueger advised. "We'll be in the field for a while, which means you'll need something to eat and cover yourself."

Handles for the bread bags followed.

"You two stay close to me at all times," the moon face explained to his shooters II and III. "When I jump, you jump. When I shoot, you keep your heads down. The barrel change has to be done in a flash, and when the ammunition belt is shot, I need supplies as fast as possible."

"All right," Wimmer replied.

Thaler nodded silently.

When we arrived at the staging area, we were given a briefing on the situation. Our battalion had been deployed alongside our comrades from Regiment 200. Our mission was to storm and take Monte Natale. The British were entrenched there.

Monte Natale was a strategically important height in the hilly landscape behind Minturno. It controlled the road to Santa Maria In-fante and Minturno, as well as the road from Formia to Ausonia on the northwest side of the hill.

The ridge was made up of karstified limestone. The slopes were overgrown with withered grass and a few gnarled olive trees. Occasionally a farmhouse with its small outbuildings could be seen on the slope.

About 800 meters southeast of Monte Natale was the relocated cemetery of Minturno, and a little further away the first roofs of some suburban houses could be seen.

Our 5th Company was on our left and had orders to clear the cemetery of the enemy while we stormed up the mountain. It was already 16:30 when we marched in line.

The II/5th had already started its attack, supported by a few tanks of the Herman Göring. A thick black mushroom cloud was rising in the sunset. Of course I hoped that it came from a burning British vehicle and not from one of our tanks. Instead of thinking too much about it, I concentrated on the road and tried not to look in the direction of the dark smoke.

We climbed up a dirt road and followed its course. At first we were surrounded by grass and bushes, typical pine and olive trees. We still felt somewhat protected. But as we looked up, it became more and more barren and rocky. The sounds of battle increased. They accompanied us from the moment we got off the trucks.

The vanguard of the company consisted of four men from Master Sergeant Semmler's platoon. It was chilly, but fortunately it wasn't raining. It would soon be dusk, so we moved quickly. Erwin Mueller was panting in front of me, carrying the MG 42 over his shoulders. Elmar Roeder walked behind me. When the path widened a little, Roeder slid in next to me. He was about to ask a question when heavy machine-gun fire started.

Rrrrrt rrrrt

"Take cover!" someone shouted.

The company scattered. Rifle fire and a second machine gun were taking a heavy toll on us. The first calls for a medic could be heard. Erwin Mueller got into position and took off the belt drum. "Now do it," he hissed to Rifleman II, who opened the ammunition box in a state of complete agitation and handed the belt unsteadily with shaking hands.

We had little cover and were literally pinned to the ground. The third platoon was behind us, and Master Sergeant Semmler's platoon was right in the middle of the British field of fire. The poor bastards took the brunt of it. The first carbines returned fire.

A light machine gun rattled away, but fell silent when both British machine guns fired on it.

"Charge!" ordered Captain Geller, who stood between us and the third platoon. "Up with you! Forward!" he shouted, chasing Lieutenant Gassner, the platoon leader of the third platoon, forward with his men.

"Attack!" thundered Master Sergeant Semmler, trying to whip his men up the hill. But every time a few Landser rose to their feet, the British machine guns drove them back into cover.

Lieutenant Kohler gave the order to attack. We stood up and inevitably came under British defensive fire. Two men immediately fell like wet sandbags.

Bullets whizzed around my ears. Down again. Take cover. Take a deep breath and overcome the inner bastard that triggers the flight animal in you. Soldiers must obey! Even if they want to run away, they can't.

"Forward!" I heard the voice of Lieutenant Gassner from behind, who had moved forward with his men.

Diagonally in front of me, Ede crouched behind a large boulder and rummaged through his binoculars. "Get ready," he called to me, peering over the rock. He pointed right and raised one finger. Then he pointed to the left and raised two fingers. I immediately understood that the two enemy machine gun nests were there and passed the information on to Erwin Mueller, who was lying slightly to my right with his two gunners and understood my shouts despite the noise of the battle. "The Bren MGs are at 10 o'clock on the left and 1 o'clock on the right!" I indicated the times by pointing with ten fingers and then with one finger.

Erwin raised his left hand briefly to show that he understood.

As two of the first platoon's machine guns hammered away to protect the advancing soldiers, hand grenades detonated near them.

Boom!

Shrapnel, dust, and rocks flew up and swirled around. When the cloud of explosions cleared, Master Sergeant Semmler jumped to his feet. "Now! Forward!" he shouted, and charged up the hill, followed by about two squads of his platoon, while the third squad fired barrages. One of the machine guns fell silent. The crew had fallen victim to a hand grenade. Cries of pain and whimpering repeatedly drowned out the din of battle.

"Mediiiiic!"

One of the wounded cried out in pain. Someone sat down beside him and struggled wildly. He was also the one desperately calling for the medics. "Mediiiic!"

"Attack!"

This order was for us. Lieutenant Kohler ran off. I hurried up and followed him.

Damn it, why isn't Erwin firing yet, I thought.

The charge uphill took strength. Krueger ran to my right. He was panting like crazy. His face was dripping with sweat.

Rrrrrrttttt

The British machine guns were hammering away again, firing their rounds in our direction. We had to take cover. I felt something hot on my head. A bullet had passed my right ear. I automatically grabbed the spot. It was bleeding slightly. My heart was racing and my pulse was pounding as I realized that I had missed the bullet by only a few millimeters.

Finally Erwin's MG 42 rattled, and with well-aimed bursts of fire he kept the British MG nest, which was the biggest threat to us, at bay.

"Go on," Kohler ordered.

I clutched my carbine and braced myself as I heard grenades whistling towards me.

Wham

I instinctively wanted to throw myself back down, but the shells flew over us and died behind us. The British artillery had fired too far. We heaved a sigh of relief. It would certainly take a few minutes for the Ari observer to instruct the gunners to shift their fire.

Rrrrt rrrrrt

Erwin fired burst after burst from his weapon. Every seventh round was a tracer. Like delicate, spinning threads, their brightly glittering tracks stretched across the terrain, only to be lost to the enemy. It helped the shooter correct the direction of his fire. While Erwin seemed to have one of the British machine-gun nests completely under control, the second began firing at him. Master Sergeant Semmler, whose attack was supported by the third platoon, took advantage of this to advance.

Boom!

The British soldiers kept throwing egg hand grenades, which exploded with a crash. The screams of the wounded grew louder and more piercing. The medics ran up the steep slope, crouching. I admired their courage. They lay down on the white armband with the red cross. That was all the protection they had, yet they moved bravely through the enemy fire. In the twilight, they were often unrecognized and shot at, just like us. It was a tragedy that took place on the slopes of Monte Natale.

Together with Kummerer and the mute, Ede had managed to get quite close to the machine gun nest, which Erwin skillfully kept at bay. Suddenly our machine gun fell silent.

Lieutenant Kohler was at my level, slightly offset from the other two groups. Lying on his back, he slid a new rod magazine into his MP 40. He rolled over, knelt down, and thrust his right fist upward. "Come on, men!"

We got up again and fought our way forward a few meters to push the Tommy over the damn ridge. This time there was heavy fire from the right. A strong group of British took cover behind large boulders and fired at us. At least two or three of the first group were badly hit. I had a good view. The magazine was empty and I pulled a loading strip out of the cartridge pouch. As I had practiced a thousand times, I slid it into the carbine and fired. The increasing darkness made it easy to see the muzzle flash. From time to time one of the plate helmets danced in front of my visor for a split second. I was on target and about to pull the trigger when someone called my name loudly.

"Old man!"

I looked back. It was Lieutenant Kohler. He was crawling belly up to me. "Give Sergeant Schwarz cover!"

The pause in fire from Erwin's MG 42 did not go unnoticed. The British MG crew reacted quickly. The barrel of their Bren machine gun was pushed over the stone cover. In an instant it rattled off and fired at our left flank. Ede was directly between the Bren and us. He was too far away to throw a grenade. The advantage of my three legionnaire comrades was that they were difficult for the enemy to see in the dim light and had not yet been discovered. At least as long as they remained motionless on the ground, they had nothing to fear. If the enemy machine gunner spotted them, they would inevitably be lost. The Bren MG was a good and very reliable weapon with high accuracy. We had learned to know and fear it in Africa.

A large part of our platoon joined me in firing on both machine gun nests. When Ede realized that the Bren crew was under pressure, he gave Kummerer and the taciturn Buchecker the appropriate hand signals. They continued to work their way forward.

Meanwhile, layer after layer of enemy shells came crashing down on us, digging into the slopes of Monte Natale. The artillery fire was not dangerous for us at the moment, but our medics, especially those carrying the wounded, had to go through this hell.

Huit - wham - wham huuiiit - wham

Captain Geller crouched by the radio operators and waved his arms wildly. A map lay in front of him. His right hand dropped to the map and his fingers danced over it, searching. Finally, the officer pointed to a few different locations. The last dim light didn't seem to be enough. He turned on his flashlight and let the beam sweep over the map while the radio operators carried out his orders. I guessed they were in contact with the battalion command post.

I refocused on the enemy, took aim and fired. After firing five well-aimed shots, I awkwardly fumbled for a new loading strip from the cartridge pouch while lying down. Each of us had two of these on our belts, each filled with 6 x 5 clips. I counted silently so as not to shoot myself and end up without ammunition. We had been taught this in the Legion and it had become second nature to all of us Legionnaires. I was also convinced that I had scored at least one hit.

Lieutenant Kohler gave the order to attack. We stood up and inevitably came under British defensive fire. Two men immediately fell like wet sandbags.

Bullets whizzed around my ears. Down again. Take cover. Take a deep breath and overcome the inner bastard that triggers the flight animal in you. Soldiers must obey! Even if they want to run away, they can't.

"Forward!" I heard the voice of Lieutenant Gassner from behind, who had moved forward with his men.

Diagonally in front of me, Ede crouched behind a large boulder and rummaged through his binoculars. "Get ready," he called to me, peering over the rock. He pointed right and raised one finger. Then he pointed to the left and raised two fingers. I immediately understood that the two enemy machine gun nests were there and passed the information on to Erwin Mueller, who was lying slightly to my right with his two gunners and understood my shouts despite the noise of the battle. "The Bren MGs are at 10 o'clock on the left and 1 o'clock on the right!" I indicated the times by pointing with ten fingers and then with one finger.

Erwin raised his left hand briefly to show that he understood.

As two of the first platoon's machine guns hammered away to protect the advancing soldiers, hand grenades detonated near them.

Boom!

Shrapnel, dust, and rocks flew up and swirled around. When the cloud of explosions cleared, Master Sergeant Semmler jumped to his feet. "Now! Forward!" he shouted, and charged up the hill, followed by about two squads of his platoon, while the third squad fired barrages. One of the machine guns fell silent. The crew had fallen victim to a hand grenade. Cries of pain and whimpering repeatedly drowned out the din of battle.

"Mediiiiic!"

One of the wounded cried out in pain. Someone sat down beside him and struggled wildly. He was also the one desperately calling for the medics. "Mediiiiiic!"

"Attack!"

This order was for us. Lieutenant Kohler ran off. I hurried up and followed him.

Damn it, why isn't Erwin firing yet, I thought.

The charge uphill took strength. Krueger ran to my right. He was panting like crazy. His face was dripping with sweat.

Rrrrrrttttt

The British machine guns were hammering away again, firing their rounds in our direction. We had to take cover. I felt something hot on my head. A bullet had passed my right ear. I automatically grabbed the spot. It was bleeding slightly. My heart was racing and my pulse was pounding as I realized that I had missed the bullet by only a few millimeters.

Finally Erwin's MG 42 rattled, and with well-aimed bursts of fire he kept the British MG nest, which was the biggest threat to us, at bay.

"Go on," Kohler ordered.

I clutched my carbine and braced myself as I heard grenades whistling towards me.

Whammm

I instinctively wanted to throw myself back down, but the shells flew over us and died behind us. The British artillery had fired too far. We heaved a sigh of relief. It would certainly take a few minutes for the Ari observer to instruct the gunners to shift their fire.

Rrrrt rrrrrt

Erwin fired burst after burst from his weapon. Every seventh round was a tracer. Like delicate, spinning threads, their brightly glittering tracks stretched across the terrain, only to be lost to the enemy. It helped the shooter correct the direction of his fire.

The charging process was completed in seconds. I fired the repeater and took aim again. With a steady hand, I took aim at the enemy, which became increasingly difficult as night fell. Suddenly there was a flicker in the sky behind us. A heavy rumbling filled the air. Shortly thereafter, we heard loud crashing and bursting among the British. Heavy suitcases hit the ridge.

Wham - wham

"Hurraaaaaaaaa," cheered our men.

The artillery supported us and was right on target.

Now all the German machine guns were hammering away at the same time. They fired barrages. Meanwhile, Ede had gotten within range of one of the British machine gun nests. He pulled a hand grenade from his belt and unscrewed the safety cap. Kummerer and Buchecker were close behind him and did the same. Again Ede gave a signal and all three pulled the release cords from the hand grenades. The Landser jumped up to get a better throwing position and threw the stick grenades in the direction of the enemy machine gun position. Immediately after the toss, while the grenades were still spinning in the air, they took cover again.

The Tommys had realized the danger too late. They were too busy firing at us and our machine guns. They were also caught off guard by the artillery fire. By the time they noticed the three Landsers in front of their position, it was too late. Rifleman I jerked the barrel of the Bren around once more and fired two short bursts that whistled close over Ede, but then there were three huge rumbles.

Wham wham wham.

Two of the grenades exploded in the immediate vicinity of the British, the third had hit and exploded right in front of Rifleman I. A picture of horror remained. The British soldier's face was barely recognizable as such, a mass of bloody pulp and bone. The machine-gun crew, crouched behind him, lay dead on the cold rocky ground, riddled with shrapnel.

After our artillery fire fell silent, we jumped up and charged. The "Hurrah!" was hard to get out. The shouting was exhausting and sapped our strength. Nevertheless, it pulled the men up and drove them forward. Their legs were heavy and sore from the march up the mountain. It was dark. Night had fallen silently and unnoticed over the land. We fired at the fading muzzle flashes of the British.

Master Sergeant Semmler's platoon had managed to penetrate the enemy position. Flares shot up into the sky. I saw tangled balls of men. Close combat. Screams. Our platoon and the III Platoon buddies were moving up. The wobbly magnesium light went out. Hands were raised. First prisoners. A few Brits fled into the darkness. Gunfire died away. We had made it and stormed the mountain. Captain Geller immediately contacted the battalion and ordered us into position.

Rumble!

There was a rumble some distance from us. Meanwhile, the British artillery had opened fire on our right flank. I felt sorry for the comrades who had taken up positions there. There was no good cover on the ridge of Monte Natale. Bare rock and rubble lay below us. We did what the Tommys had done and collected larger rocks, which we arranged in a semicircle to form a kind of wall. But the protection was more of a psychological nature. It wouldn't have been able to withstand actual attacks from the Ari.

Guards were assigned and outposts were sent into the area. One group helped the medics transport the wounded. Since the ridge was impassable for the Sankas, the poor fellows had to be carried on stretchers to the next larger casualty collection point in the valley, from where they were transported to the field hospital. The porters were panting under the load, and more than once one of them tripped or stumbled in the rough terrain. It was the wounded who suffered, screaming loudly as they fell to the hard ground with the stretcher.

The British prisoners were taken to the battalion command post. Fallen soldiers from both sides were recovered as best they could by torchlight. They were placed in paper bags and the bodies were also taken to a sort of collection point. They were to be buried in daylight with due decorum.

It was just before midnight when the Tommy again tried to break in on the right flank with a strong raiding party. Perhaps their goal was to take prisoners for interrogation. The attack was repulsed.

Around 1 a.m. I finally managed to eat something. Commis bread and tinned sausage. God knows I would have given anything for something warm to eat. The wind was whistling around our ears and it was terribly cold on the ridge of Monte Natale.

Happy not to be assigned to the outpost or to guard duty, I wrapped myself in the canvas tent after my meager meal and tried to fall asleep. The rumble of the guns slowly subsided and the agonizing screams and cries of the wounded were no longer audible. A few cigarette burns, hidden in cupped hands, could be seen in the darkness. Completely exhausted, I fell into a light, restless sleep.

"Parole?" I heard someone call out and opened my eyes.

It was dawn and I was exhausted. It was cold. Shivering, I pulled the canvas far up over my nose.

"Boy, put that iron away. If you don't recognize your spit by the sound of it, I'll take you sledding in the next exercise," Sergeant Major Klemm's voice thundered at the poor boy.

I immediately stuck my head out of the canvas and looked

over the edge. Sure enough. Our spit was running ahead of the men of the supply train. Groaning slightly and glad to have made the climb, a handful of men followed. They were packed full of food containers strapped to their backs like backpacks. They also had packs and thermos flasks strapped to their backs.

"Excuse me, Sergeant Major," the grenadier in question replied reverently. He was one of the new recruits.

"That's all right, boy. You were right to ask who was approaching," he said in a conciliatory tone.

The group passed the guard.

Captain Geller was already on his feet and had noticed the Company Sergeant's arrival. He walked straight up to him. "Klemm, what brings you here?"

"I took the liberty of organizing a hot breakfast for the company. I thought a little exercise early in the morning wouldn't hurt," the spitfire grinned. "I rounded up the men from the troop. That way the food runners don't have to march down and up again. It saved time, Captain."

The company commander grinned and shook his head. "If I hadn't been looking forward to a hot cup of coffee, I would have bundled you up. You had orders to take care of the wounded."

"Everything is under control, Captain. The wounded are being tended to."

Geller nodded approvingly and patted Klemm on the shoulder. "Well done."

For the first time, I felt I recognized something human in both men.

Spit turned around. "Distribute the food containers in batches. And the men are to make sure that everyone gets so-and-so when they pass it out. There's no more than that."

I undressed from the blanket and canvas and grabbed the cooking utensils lying beside me. The line was still short, but more and more Landser were streaming toward the food counter.

"Remember the outposts," I heard someone yell.

The coffee was no longer hot, but at least it was lukewarm. Contrary to my expectations, it was strong, tasted strong, and woke me up with the first sip. The soup was only slightly steaming in the cold morning air when it was ladled into the pot. Unfortunately, it was also lukewarm. But that didn't matter. It tasted great and drove the night's chill out of my body.

It was getting lighter and lighter. A short distance away from my night camp, I was cleaning my cooking utensils with some water from my canteen. When I had poured the last of the liquid out of the container and wiped everything dry with my handkerchief, I went back to my relatively uncomfortable camp-site. There I rolled up the blanket and tent sheet and tied them up neatly.

I'm sure they'll let us start right away, or at least give us some orders or information, I thought to myself.

Elmar Roeder, who had camped beside me for the night, asked what time it was. "My watch has stopped," he added.

My left arm moved in front of my chest. The sleeve of my coat slipped back, exposing the watch on my wrist. Memories flooded through me. I loved that old watch. It was a gift from my grandfather, who had bought it after a trip to Switzerland. "Take good care of it, son. It's precise and didn't come cheap," he warned me at the time. It was my fourteenth birthday and I was proud as a peacock. My next thought was of the family grave and the names on the tombstone came to mind. I was over-come with sadness and wondered if I would ever see Robert's grave in Russia. All we had was a photo of it. It was a birch cross with a wooden plaque bearing his name. Behind it you could va-guely make out other graves. I thought of my other brother. Oskar! I wonder how he's doing? I hoped he would recover from his wound and come home.

"And?" I was torn from my thoughts. "What time is it?"
I cleared my throat. "Exactly 7 o'clock!"
Huiiiit!

I didn't like this whistling at all. Instinctively, I threw myself onto the stony ground. "Get down!" I shouted. My warning had barely been uttered when I heard a crash.

Thud!

The earth around us began to shake and tremble. It thundered, cracked and flashed incessantly. It was as if Monte Natale was shaking to throw us off its back.

Huiiit ... wham

Explosive mushrooms shot up, sending shrapnel, rocks and dirt flying with them. Shrapnel whirled through our position at deadly speed, drilling into everything in its path. Some comrades tried desperately to dig a foxhole with a folding spade, but our nighttime observation was confirmed by daylight: digging was impossible on this ridge. The ground was rocky. The only option was to lie flat on the ground and huddle together.

Huiiit ... wham

I made myself as small as possible and crouched in the embriole position behind my 40 to 50 cm high wall of piled stones. I was powerless. I was helpless. I was doomed to die. Anyone who jumped up to escape was inevitably torn to pieces by shrapnel or blown to pieces by a grenade. A thousand things were running through my mind. Sometimes, as a little boy, I ran around the circus tent, sometimes I sat on my mother's lap and cried because my brothers were bigger and stronger. I remembered my first kiss, but also my basic training in the Legion. Again and again, the impact of the shells would rip me from my thoughts and bring me back to this cruel reality.

I didn't want to die. I felt weak and trembled like a leaf. If I hadn't done my morning toilette just before the artillery fire, I would have definitely been lying there with my pants full. It was a game of life and death. The Grim Reaper rode through our ranks laughing, swinging his scythe, and whoever looked at him was taken on an eternal journey to the afterlife.

One of the grenades exploded very close to us. I felt the shock wave of the detonation. Shards of stone rained down on me. I lay petrified and covered my ears. I moved all my limbs one by one. First my fingers, then my hands, followed by my toes, feet and joints. Miraculously, I was completely unharmed. I blinked and looked over at Elmar Roeder. He also seemed to be unharmed, but there was a torn off hand right in front of his head. It had just landed there. Tendons, shreds of bloody flesh and skin could be seen around the exposed bone. Elmar was white as a sheet, jerked back and vomited immediately. I closed my eyes again.

Huiiiit ... wham

The blows receded a little. But the shelling continued with full force. This time the slope behind us was the target of the British artillery. We continued to lie motionless on the ground. The inevitable happened. The wounded began to moan and scream. The calls for medics grew louder and louder. I dared to lift my head. The air was filled with a gray haze, a mixture of dust and gun smoke. Breathing scratched my throat. With the light, cold wind blowing from the sea, the haze slowly dissipated.

"Meeeediiiic!"

"Medic! Over here!"

"Ahhh ... ahhh."

It was terrible and nothing could compare. The artillery attack lasted exactly 30 minutes. At 7:30 a.m., the British guns suddenly fell silent. The standard military procedure began immediately.

"Attention! Remain in position. The reserve group will support the medics! Where are the wounded?" shouted one of the squad leaders.

Captain Geller immediately contacted the outpost. We feared an infantry attack after the artillery barrage. We were relieved when the report came through that there were no Tommys on the advance.

Recruit Thaler from our group had been badly wounded. A shell had almost severed his left leg below the knee. He was screaming like crazy and hitting the ground with the stump, completely shocked. Blood splattered everywhere. The mute held Thaler tight. Kummerer, the trained butcher, looked first at the giant Buchecker, then at Ede, who had now joined him. The mute shook his head. Ede also said: "That can't be mended. Do it!"

Now I knew what Kummerer was trying to achieve with his look. He wanted to have his opinion confirmed and to get permission to cut the last tendons and muscle cords. The Palatine pulled out his combat knife, sharper than a razor blade, and applied it. A few quick cuts followed, which Thaler hadn't really noticed. His lower leg rolled a few centimeters to the side. Roeder, still pale from the severed hand, immediately turned to the side and choked again. One of the paramedics appeared. He gave Thaler a tetanus shot and pushed a morphine tablet into his mouth. Then he sprinkled the stump with wound powder and bandaged it with nimble hands. "There are no free bands. He'll have to wait," he hurried on, completely overwhelmed.

The mute just shook his head, stood up and picked up Thaler. He held the wounded man in his arms as if he were a small child. "He must go to the military hospital at once. I'll carry him down."

That was a day's worth of words for Buchecker. Without waiting for Ede's approval, he marched off.

Lieutenant Kohler came running to us. He saw the mute disappear. "Why aren't you at your posts? Where's Buchecker going?"

Ede cleared his throat. "He's assisting the medics. If Thaler doesn't get to the hospital as soon as possible, he has little chance of survival."

"Damn! There's another group supporting the medics. How dare you..."

"I gave him the order, Lieutenant," Ede lied, trying to protect the mute's actions.

Kohler blew in and out vigorously. "Our platoon was

exempted from guard duty because we were assigned to a shock troop. The artillery attack set us back in time. The new orders are to wait and see. But we're moving out by 9 a.m. at the latest. We have to find out where the Tommy lines are. If Buchecker isn't back by then, there will be consequences. We are beaten and need every man."

"He'll be back," replied Ede.

Kohler was furious, but he could understand the mute's behavior. I was glad that our leading officer hadn't completely shed his human side in the war. "To your posts!" he ordered.

To make up for Thaler's absence at the machine gun, Ede assigned Elmar Roeder, who still looked a bit batty, as the new Rifleman III. "The machine gun is our heaviest and most important weapon," he explained. "You knock us out when we need cover, shoot barrage fire when we attack or retreat, and if you are well positioned, you can keep even a numerically superior opponent under control with your firepower."

Roeder understood the explanation. "Yes, Sergeant."

Ede grinned. "We agreed a long time ago that we'd all be on a first-name basis in the group. They really drilled it into you to be on first-name terms in the barracks."

"Yes, Serg..., uh," Roeder improved, "Ede."

Our third platoon was in the middle of the Ari attack and the Tommys had more or less shot it to pieces. Captain Geller disbanded the platoon and distributed the few men who could still fight among the rest of the company.

We were assigned the light grenade launcher squad. Seven men were assigned to the other two squads. The rest of the 3rd Platoon was integrated into Master Sergeant Semmler's platoon.

This gave our company two strong platoons.

The mute was back just before 9 o'clock. He was drenched in sweat, didn't say a word and sat down. I assumed that he had met porters on the way who had taken the badly wounded man from him. Pocke, on the other hand, offered a wager. He believed that Buchecker had walked all the way to the collection point in the valley and back again. That would be a record. None of us agreed to the wager, however, because the mute would have to be trusted. The giant of a man kept his mouth shut.

Wimmer handed Buchecker a canteen, which the former shepherd gratefully accepted. His clumsy hands gripped it. He tapped it, and you could hear it gurgle. His Adam's apple moved up and down. The bottle was empty in an instant. Buchecker handed it back and gave a quick nod. That was his way of saying thank you.

Less than five minutes later, Lieutenant Kohler joined us. He noted favorably that Buchecker was back and said nothing about his good Samaritan act. He turned to Ede. "Sergeant Schwarz, get ready for the assault team."

Kohler left, Ede stood up. "Comrades, you've heard. Stand up and check your weapons. If you want to smoke a cigarette, this is your last chance. Be ready to march in five minutes."

We headed for Minturno. Our platoon was assigned two of the three signalmen in the company. One of them was also trained as a sniper. Snipers were primarily used to fight the enemy by eliminating tactical targets while applying psychological pressure. They were also used to provide security during advance and retreat, and to protect the flanks of reconnaissance units. In addition to the signalmen, we were accompanied by three intelligence soldiers who lined up at the rear with their equipment. Lieutenant Kohler had joined the shock troop of Master Sergeant Semmler.

The light mortar squad remained in position.

The war had reared its ugly head once again. When you were caught in the drumfire, you were helpless. You could pray, sing, laugh, or do anything, but you couldn't run. Whether you fell victim to the attack or survived unscathed was always left to chance. Fate played a cruel game with us.

Pictures of Thaler kept appearing before my eyes. Yesterday he marched beside us as a healthy young man. Today he was a cripple who had lost his lower leg. A war invalid, they called him. Just like that. Just because he happened to be lying next to a dying grenade. The fatherland will thank him with a crutch and, if he is lucky, a prosthesis. To get through life, he will get a few marks in disability pension.

I shook my head and wanted to shake the images out of my mind - like a wet dog shaking the water out of its fur after a bath.

Drumfire was pure hell and just about the worst thing that could happen to a soldier in war. There was only one thing I found more terrifying than lying helpless in a hail of enemy fire: Close combat. When you stood face to face with your opponent, knowing that a duel to the death was imminent. Him against you. Two men who had never met in their lives, charging at each other to kill each other. It was unparalleled in terms of psychological cruelty.

The headmaster's voice snapped me out of my thoughts.

"Follow the line."

Our troop marched in unison. Our mission was to scout the area and, if possible, take prisoners. Lieutenant Kohler said the battalion was preparing an attack to reinforce the breach in the Gustav Line.

After we had walked a good distance and left the ridge on the side of the mountain facing the enemy, we heard another rumble behind us. Once again, our position on Monte Natale was under heavy British artillery fire.

"Poor bastards," Krueger hissed.

I wondered why someone like him would cut short his vacation only to end up back here in the hell of war.

Because of the massive artillery fire, we suspected a preparatory attack by the British, followed by an assault to regain the strategically important heights.

Ede sent Kummerer, the sniper, and Krueger forward as scouts. "We will stay on this path and advance in a straight line.

As soon as the British appear, we'll switch to a firing line and you stay in the middle with the machine gun," he said, pointing to Erwin Mueller, who carried the MG 42 with a belt at his side, ready to fire. A belt drum was attached.

I was glad not to be in the middle of the artillery fire again, but I also didn't feel comfortable in the rocky and almost un-covered terrain. When we were finally surrounded by some trees, I felt safer. The artillery fire of the Tommys decreased with time and finally stopped completely. Wordlessly, trying to make as little noise as possible, we moved forward. Step by step. Our eyes scanned the area. If the enemy had positioned snipers, we would surely be easy prey. The first to be hit would be the head-master. The leaders were favorite targets. Ede knew this. I admi-red him all the more. I wondered if I would be as determined as the headmaster. The thought made me feel queasy.

Think again, I reminded myself. Concentrate on the area!

I was surrounded by a kind of inner silence. It went hand in hand with highly concentrated observation of my surroundings and also with fear. Despite the daylight, our advance into enemy territory reminded me of the night reconnaissance missions in Africa. Goose bumps formed on the back of my neck and an un-pleasant, indescribable feeling spread. It reminded me of a long-ago experience.

As children, we were playing in a forest and discovered a cave. Full of adventure, we crawled through the narrow entrance and ventured inside. The darker and colder it got, the more frigh-tened I became. I felt watched and helpless. I felt the same way about the scouting party at that moment.

Where the path had once wound its way through rocky and stony terrain, now it led through withered grassland, overgrown with gnarled olive trees. I wondered how old they were and be-gan to see something beautiful in this stretch of land.

The sun was hidden behind a gray cloud cover and it was still cold. I was glad that the company sergeant had provided a hot breakfast. The thought of it made me forget for a moment the danger we were in. Except for the clatter of equipment banging against each other, it was quiet. Except for a few quiet curses from the moon face every now and then. The machine gun was unwieldy, weighing over eleven kilos with the belt drum. Beads of sweat ran down his fiery red face.

I was all the more shocked when the dull whip of a few shots shattered the silence. Ede raised his right arm and stopped immediately. Signs followed that we should spread out. The group split up and took cover. It wasn't long before we saw a Landser running towards us. It was Krueger. A few more volleys rang out, then the fire died down.

We watched Kruger move with remarkable agility. Ready for possible fire support, we had set up and AI-meded the area behind our comrade. There were no British soldiers in sight. Krueger was obviously not being pursued. He was panting wildly as he stood in front of the Chief Instructor and rattled off his report. "Tommies! A big scouting party. They saw me, but not the other two. We moved to the side. When there was a bang, Kummerer and the sniper immediately took cover. They told me to run to you and warn you.

The soldier's chest rose and fell quickly. He flinched as a single shot rang out. The echo echoed through the compound. We assumed the sniper had hit. I got goose bumps again and a sinking feeling spread through my stomach. Killing in battle was one evil, targeting an enemy through a telescopic sight and pulling the trigger was another.

Ede didn't think twice. He knew what to do. "Forward. We attack," he ordered.

We moved forward in a firing line. Each of us had his rifle ready to fire, Erwin held the MG 42 at waist level. Roeder and Wimmer, his marksmen II and III, were close behind.

Krueger took the lead with Ede and showed us the way. After only a few hundred meters he continued in a crouched position and then stopped a little further on. "Tommy can see us from here," he warned, sinking to the ground and crawling through the terrain on all fours.

There had been silence since the last single shot.

Had our sniper fired?

Each of us knew there could be two reasons for the silence. Either the Tommys had retreated, or they were so cautious that they didn't fire into the blind, but waited and scouted the area. If that was the case, we had to be very careful not to be ambushed.

After another 40 or 50 meters, Krueger stopped. Ede gave us tactical signals to spread out across the terrain. I didn't know where he was coming from, but suddenly Kumme-rer was standing with the chief instructor, gesticulating wildly with his hands. He pointed straight ahead and several times to the right. I guessed the British were there.

Ede came around the back and waved us together. We knelt down under a large olive tree.

"The Tommys can't see us here," he began, and then instructed the reconnaissance soldiers to contact the company CP. There followed a flurry of work on the radios. As the coils and wires heated up, we were briefed on the situation. The Schoolmaster split the platoon in two. His tactics were simple: he wanted to attack the enemy on both flanks, while Erwin was to fight the Tommys head-on with continuous fire from his MG 42, confusing them completely.

The two judges, another young comrade whose name I didn't know, and I were to stay with Erwin and his two riflemen. Moonface was of the opinion that Wimmer was enough for him as second shooter. Elmar Roeder was to stay with me. "When the machine-gun barrel glows and needs to be changed, you'll make a real racket," he said.

The sniper was supposed to cover the attack from a safe position.

There wasn't much time to think. Ede gave the order to fire immediately after his speech. Erwin took position, replaced the belt drum with an ammunition belt, silently closed the breech and signaled readiness to fire. At the same time, our two attack wedges moved forward.

Erwin's eyes slid over the cold steel of the weapon. He aimed at the area where we suspected the enemy to be. Short breaths. His cheeks glowed red. The machine-gunner was focused. With the crook of his right forefinger, the machine gun rattled away.

Rrrt ... rrrrt

The belt slid smoothly. Sleeve after sleeve danced in the air. Each one spun around its own axis several times before landing on the cold earth. Muzzle flashes flickered from the barrel. Projectiles hurtled toward the invisible enemy with deadly effect. The firepower of the MG 42 was enormous. It almost seemed as if Erwin had the entire room in front of us under control.

Rrrt ... rrt

Nothing moved on the other side. An eerie silence. The lack of return fire led me to believe that the enemy had long since retreated and that we were attacking an unoccupied area. I imagined fun evenings of camaraderie where I could tease Ede about having attacked and defeated an imaginary enemy. I was so sure that there was no British soldier ahead of us that I was inclined to drop my guard and stand up.

The machine gun was silent. The belt was empty. Erwin pulled the gun back. Wimmer had a new belt ready. In a few moments it was inserted and the MG 42 was ready to fire again. The moment Erwin reloaded the barrel, a few hand grenades went off and a firefight broke out. While the left attack group was under heavy fire, I heard our comrades screaming from the right. Erwin pulled the trigger and the machine gun went off again.

The rest of us pushed our carbines forward and looked for targets. Unlike before, I saw muzzle flashes. At one point I thought I saw an Englishman pointing his rifle at our machine gun. His metal helmet was clearly visible. I fired two shots and then the helmet was gone.

"Change the barrel!" the moon face suddenly squealed. The

machine gun suddenly fell silent. Erwin and his Gunner II worked quickly, while the rest of us fired fast and rather aimlessly in the direction of the Tommys.

"Done!"

As the machine gun was ready to fire again and rattled away, the sound of battle abruptly subsided and finally fell silent.

"Wait!" I called to Erwin.

We looked at each other. We nodded at each other. The machine gun was silent.

The cheers grew louder. It was the redemptive hurrah. The shout you gave when the battle was won and you weren't one of those left on the battlefield.

"Hurraaaa!" it rang out from Roeder's lips, too. Softly at first, then louder and louder and finally at the top of his voice.

Looking at my young comrade, I saw relief on his face. His fear had given way to a small euphoria of victory. I thought for a moment about telling him that this wasn't a real battle, just a small taste of the hell of war, but I didn't.

We had taken two prisoners. The two Brits were slightly wounded but able to walk. You could see the fear in their faces. One of our men offered them a cigarette. One Tommy shook his head, the other accepted.

One of our comrades had been killed, two soldiers wounded. One of them had a huge lump on his head that threatened to burst. The butt of an English rifle had thundered against the man's skull.

"A normal skull would split open from the force of such a blow, the medic told me. I know I have a wooden head, but I didn't think it would be so stable," he tried to joke when he noticed that we were all looking at the strangely swollen shape of his head. "Does anyone have another aspirin for me?" he added.

The second injured man was the sniper. A grenade fragment had torn almost the entire eyebrow above his right eye. He looked like his face had been dipped in a pot of red paint. The medic had painstakingly bandaged the soldier's eye, covering it almost completely.

As we marched off, Pocke, the mute, and two of the young recruits fell back. They formed the rear guard. It would have been the sniper's job to cover the retreat, but the bandage over his eye ruined his mission.

I joined him. The snipers, as we used to call them, were always suspicious of us regular infantrymen. We feared them, didn't like them, but were glad to have them in our ranks because their presence meant safety. I couldn't really explain why they were shunned. Probably because they had a reputation for being cold and ruthless.

"There's a difference between firing a machine gun into a mass of charging soldiers and looking at the enemy's face in the scope and then pulling the trigger," someone once told me. "You have to be cold to do that. Freezing cold!"

Those words echoed through my mind. I wondered what the war had done to us. Was I still the young circus performer inside looking for adventure, or had I become a tool of an army? I wondered if I had killed or wounded a British soldier today. Again my eyes fell on the soldier marching beside me. His rifle was shouldered. He had removed the sight. He knew for sure if he had scored any hits and how many. I studied the sniper for a long time. Tens of questions formed in my head, but I didn't dare speak to him.

"What do you want to know?" he asked suddenly and unexpectedly.

The situation embarrassed me. I cleared my throat. "It looks bad," I replied, pointing at the bandage.

What a coward I was. Why didn't I ask him to answer all my questions?

"Just a scratch." His right hand went up. He ran his fingers carefully over the bandage. "I won't be able to shoot for a few days."

"How's that?" I was startled by my question and regretted it

the moment I asked it. I wanted to sink into the ground. I hoped
he overheard it, in which case I would retreat a bit in silence. I'd
heard once that snipers don't talk about what they do, and that
they react very pessimistically when asked about it.
"What?"

He turned and looked at me. "Foreign Legion?" he finally
added.
I nodded.
"Far East? South America?"
"North Africa."
The sniper took note of my answer, but didn't react further,
remaining silent for a minute or two.
"You want to know what it's like to kill someone specifi-
cally?"
I nodded, but didn't quite agree with his interpretation of the
question. "I want to know what it's like when you put the rifle on
and your target comes into view."
He studied me with his left eye. "If you were in the Legion,
you served in the 361st Infantry Regiment." Without waiting for
confirmation, he went on. "I don't know exactly where you served in the Foreign Legion, but I've heard some nasty stories
about their operations and procedures. You took quite a beating
from the locals in Morocco and I don't know where else, and you
were anything but squeamish. Regiment 361 was the fire depart-
ment of the German Afrika Korps at the front. You fought to the
end." He pulled a pack of Eckstein from his breast pocket, pulled
out one of the filterless cigarettes and put it between his lips. The
pack went back and a storm lighter appeared between his fingers.
A quick turn of the ignition wheel. The spark jumped to the gaso-
line-soaked wick and a blue-yellow flame danced in the wind.
He lit the cigarette, and with the first puff, the glow of the bright
orange embers could be seen. The sniper blew out the bluish
smoke and began to speak. "I was on those night patrols too. The

first time I had to thrust a bayonet into a Tommy's torso. Although the word thrust is wrong. We fought with our fists, choked and bit each other. He was a young red-haired guy. We rolled back and forth. When I got back on top, he had grabbed a rock and smashed it against my skull. Luckily I was wearing my steel helmet. At that moment, one of my hands was free. I pulled out my bayonet and plunged it into his chest. He caught my hand and only the tip of the bayonet went through. I put all my weight on the stabbing weapon. He was gasping and his eyes were wide open. As the bayonet went deeper and deeper into him, he began to squeal like a pig. He kept screaming, "No ... no ... mercy ..... That means mercy," he translated. "I don't know how long the struggle lasted. It felt like an eternity. Eventually, my body weight was stronger than his strength. When it left him, I ran the bayonet through him. He let out a piercing scream. Screams you never forget for the rest of your life. And he struggled under me for a long time. I probably hadn't pierced any arteries or vital organs. At some point, I couldn't stand the moaning anymore, so I grabbed a rock and hit him on the head until he was quiet. After that, I literally puked my guts out. That, my boy, is why I became a sniper. I know that as a soldier I have to kill when I go into battle. But I never want to have to kill anyone with my bare hands again. And if you want to know how I feel when I pull the trigger, I can only give you one answer. Ever since that night in the desert, I've hardly slept a night without thinking of that red-haired Englishman. In contrast, the faces of the men in my sights are blurred, distorted, or nonexistent. The Tommy from Africa is always there. Is that what you wanted to hear?

I was speechless. I had expected anything but that answer. He took a drag on his cigarette and blew out the smoke in puffs. Minutes passed and the sniper had long since extinguished the cigarette when I said: "I feel the same way. I mean, the faces of the men I had to kill in close combat. I often see them in front of me at night."

From a distance the artillery rumbled again. It rumbled and

thundered as if a heavy storm was brewing.

"We all have our own baggage to carry, my boy. We all have our own."

I thought about the sniper's words the rest of the way. The cloudy gray weather matched the cold, wet rock of Monte Natale. It was cold and uncomfortable. I hoped very much that we would be taken away when we returned and dreamed of a warm place to stay.

I wonder if the quartermaster had managed this feat and found shelter.

My breakfast was long gone and my stomach was growing. So my thoughts turned to the field kitchen and I could literally see the steaming cauldrons in front of me. I would have loved to have a hearty stew with meat or sausage or a goulash in the pot today. It would have been just the thing for this weather. Our company cook was a master of his trade. Whatever came out of his pot tasted good. Here, too, the hand of our new division commander, Major General Ernst-Günther Baade, could be felt. Since he was in charge, there was always good food.

We reached the position and the disappointment was great. When we returned, our section of the position on Monte Natale was just as cold, dark and empty as it had been in the early morning. The artillery fire increased and the enemy pressed along the entire front line in an attempt to break through.

We were far from being pushed to the rear. Nor did we find any steaming kettles or food carriers with hot food. There wasn't even a hot drink like tea or coffee. We were told that the supply route was right in the middle of the Allied cannon and artillery fire. My dream burst like a soap bubble.

The two prisoners were taken away for interrogation. We had a half hour break, then we were told to expand our positions and dig in.

Erwin cursed like a reed sparrow. His face glowed like an

erupting volcano. Nevertheless, he followed Captain Geler's orders and positioned himself with the MG 42 at a strategically chosen spot.

We now knew that opposite us was the 5th British Infantry Division, with the 13th, 15th and 17th Brigades in our section.

Over the next few days, the gates to the Devil's Kingdom were thrown wide open. The British tried with all their might to retake Monte Natale, but we resisted. The allied artillery barrages were hell. We Legionnaires were used to a lot. Especially in North Africa, as firemen of the DAK, we were always in the front line and thus in the hail of enemy shells. However, nothing we had endured up to that point was comparable to the artillery fire we were exposed to here on the Gustav Line.

The entrenchment work turned out to be torture. The karst limestone was impenetrable to our spades. So we had no choice but to use some of the craters that the Tommys' heavy suitcases had blasted into the rock. Although the word "craters" wasn't really appropriate here, "small depressions" was the more appropriate term.

The English, who had been here before us, had used sandbags, which we immediately put to good use. We largely dispensed with the rocks we had placed around our positions the night before in case of an infantry attack. They had proven to be extremely dangerous when hit by shells, as they would literally be blown away under sufficient pressure and thus become deadly projectiles.

In spite of the cold, I didn't freeze. The exercise had kept me warm. I was done and looked at my little work with satisfaction.

A reinforced squad was getting ready to move out. The battalion still feared an imminent infantry attack. The outposts were to be double manned and the area patrolled again. The coils of the rearguard radios, which had been frantically fiddling with switches and buttons, were still hot when our supplies arrived. I hadn't expected this and was pleased to find large containers of food next to boxes of ammunition. Commissary sandwiches were sticking out of the bags.

I still didn't like our company commander because I didn't like him. There are people you like and people you don't like. He was definitely in the second category. Nevertheless, he had my full respect for two things: He led the troops in battle from the front and didn't hide in his command post. And he made sure he had enough supplies. Rations were as important as ammunition. In my opinion, the fact that he thought of both things spoke volumes about his leadership.

Supplies were distributed first by train and then by group. When it was our turn, our eyes lit up like children under a Christmas tree in anticipation of hot food.

First, Ede handed out boxes of ammunition and boxes of hand grenades. The hand grenades were to be assembled and ready for use immediately after the meal.

The food containers contained potato soup with a good amount of meat. There was also a sandwich for every two men. Each of us also received a box of fuel tablets for our Esbit stoves, a bag of sour bread, two bags of soup concentrate, two cans of sausage, a tube of cheese, and two cans of canned food. One fish, one meat. There were also some market goods, and I grabbed a can of Schoka-Kola and a few drops. The smokers were happy to get cigarettes or tobacco, and each of us could soak our storm lighters in gasoline. There were also matches.

"Enjoy yourselves. Bon appétit," the supply sergeant wished us. A few minutes later he gathered his team and gave the order to march back. He seemed to be in a hurry to get out of here.

I was the last to get my share and was extremely lucky. Probably because of our losses, there was a whole commissary loaf left over, which was given to me with a wink. "Sometimes it pays to be last," the older comrade grinned, grabbed an empty knapsack and other supplies that were lying around, and quickly followed his sergeant.

My provisions were stowed in the knapsack. The young Geb-hardt was waiting for me. He was squatting beside a hand-grenade box and shoving a piece of bread into his mouth.

"We can go," I said, pointing to the box of hand grenades. "For us to carry?"

Gebhardt shrugged, then nodded. "Erwin took the box with the 15 grenades. He said he would carry the thing alone, which weighed just under 18 kg, and that we should carry the wooden crate in pairs."

I grinned. The box with the 15 grenades was made of sheet iron and weighed just under 18 kg. The wooden crate, on the other hand, contained 16 stick grenades and weighed about 25 kg due to the massive packaging. "Come on then. I'm hungry."

Gebhardt shoved another piece of bread into his mouth, wiped his hands on his pants legs and stood up. We grabbed the crate by the straps, lifted it up and started walking.

The background noise still consisted of orders being given, with snatches of words that were sometimes clearer and some-times less so. The soldiers without orders sat around and chatted while they enjoyed their hot meal. In addition to the men's mut-tering, there was the typical clatter of spoons being dipped into pots and scraped across the floor to get even the smallest bit of potato soup.

Not a minute later, the wind from the sea brought a hideous, muffled sound to us. It was the dreaded rumble and thunder of artillery guns. And again, only a split second later, the first shells whistled and hissed above our heads, their trajectories deep red and detonating as they hit the rocky ground.

Huiiit - wham - wham - huiiit wham

Explosive mushrooms shot up. I felt a hard blow to my up-per arm as I was thrown to the ground and feared that I had been hit by shrapnel. As I lay on the ground and crouched down, I felt the wound. Nothing bloody - probably stone chips, I realized with relief. This is going to leave a massive bruise.

Grenades raced through the air incessantly, trying to find their way to us. The bursting of the bullets rang in our ears. Thick, billowing clouds of powdery smoke made it hard to breathe and burned our lungs.

I lifted my head a little and looked around desperately for cover. One of the wagons in the supply column took a direct hit. Splinters of wood flew like arrows. One of the iron wheels had landed on a soldier lying under cover, breaking his back.

Huiiit - wham

The impact caused an excessive amount of dust and rock fragments to fall on me. My vision was completely blocked for a moment. I had to get out of here, I needed proper cover. It was clear to me that we were in the center of this Ari attack.

Two grenades rarely hit the same spot, it flashed through my mind.

"Get out of here," I yelled at Gebhardt.

He obviously couldn't hear me. Hunched over with his arms crossed, he lay on the ground next to me, two arm's length away.

The cloud of dust from the last big impact was dissipating a bit. Cracks and flashes. Three or four smaller explosions made me jump again. I waited in fear for a shower of shrapnel. When none came, I lifted my head again. The dust cloud had dissipated thanks to the wind. It was like looking through a dirty, dusty filter, but at least you could see everything clearly. There was a depression only about thirty paces diagonally in front of us.

We'll find shelter there, it shot through me.

I rolled once around my body axis and came to rest next to Gebhardt. I called his name, put my hand on the young soldier's shoulder and shook him. He screamed in pain.

"Ah... Ahhhhh!"

That didn't sound good. My comrade seemed apathetic. "Gebhardt, where did it get you?" I shouted to drown out the noise. My voice was raised in panic.

There was no answer to my screaming question. I grabbed

his body and tried to free one of his hands by pulling on his elbow. I wanted to help him get up so I could support him as he walked. The arm didn't give an inch. The hands in front of Gebhardt's body were locked together.

He started screaming and didn't stop. I lifted my upper body and bent over the wounded man. The sight I saw was horrible. Gebhard was lying on the ground with his belly open. His hands were covered in blood and were pushing the protruding intestines back into his stomach. For a moment the disgusting stench drowned out the pungent gun smoke. The screeching of the shells mingled more and more with the screams of the dying young soldier. It was only then that I noticed the pool of blood where Gebhardt lay. I assumed that a large piece of shrapnel had torn through his entire abdominal wall.

Maybe if we had gone off two or three seconds earlier or later, it wouldn't have hit him. Or maybe it would have torn open my stomach or my back.

Somewhere near the enemy, when a howitzer was fired, a shell was sent in our direction with a muzzle flash at the end of the barrel, a heavy shell was ejected, and the recoil was caught by a gun carriage. Whistling and howling, it mixed with the hellish noise of the howling explosives to detonate here with the aim of destroying all life around the impact crater.

Metallic clicks as the breeches opened, scraping noises as the loaders inserted another shell, and the gunner cranking violently as he readjusted would probably be the next steps of the operating crew. A Tommy, probably with the rank of Sergeant, would give the order to fire and the whole process would repeat itself to become part of the great roller of fire that unleashed itself upon us like a storm of steel.

"Ahhh..."

Gebhardt's agonizing cries of pain dragged me back to the present.

Huiiit - wham!

I ducked down and instinctively put my upper body over

my companion's face. Stones rained down on us again. Something sharp scraped against my helmet. I had to get out of here, but I didn't want to leave the young man alone. I was desperate. "Damn war!" I groaned, not noticing the tears streaming down my cheeks and the mucus dripping from my nose. Instinctively, I wiped them with my sleeve.

The next layer rushed over us and hit us with a thunderous crash.

Huiiit - wham ... huiiit - wham

Strong arms grabbed my shoulders. "Get out of here!" I heard Buchecker's voice. As if I were a small child, his strong arm lifted me up.

"I have to stay with Gebhardt," I croaked. My voice broke. I spat as I spoke frantically.

"Dead!"

That one word sent goose bumps all over my body. My stomach tightened and nausea crept up. I choked down the liquid in my stomach that I was about to vomit. The mute began to walk, pulling me along. I stumbled at first, but he held me so tightly that I did not fall to the ground. I took a last look at Gebhardt. He was lying there, not moving, the screaming had stopped. I didn't know if he was already dead. I had a guilty conscience, I felt miserable and empty.

The impact on the rocky ground was hard and sobering. The mute lay beside me, panting. He pulled up his legs and made himself small, as far as one could say with his stature. I saw that he had not only dragged me with him, but also the box of grenades. It lay at his feet. Buchecker had probably seen us and noticed that I was sitting upright in a state of shock next to the badly wounded man. He didn't hesitate a moment to save me.

Example Photo
soldiers-7662300_1920
Pixabay Lizenz: https://pixabay.com/de/service/license/

Silently, I lifted my legs and pressed myself against the cold stone. I didn't think about anything, just closed my eyes and waited until the bursting, howling and thundering was over.

After the shelling, they came. Infantrymen streamed up the slope. I worked without thinking. We lay side by side, aiming, firing and reloading.

At one point a group of Tommies had managed to infiltrate our position. Ede emptied the magazine of his submachine gun into the torso of the first two British soldiers. Roeder shot a British soldier standing in front of him and struck him with the butt of his rifle. The mute split one attacker's skull by striking him hard in the face with a sharpened spade. Our uniforms were covered with dirt, dust and blood.

The attack was repulsed and the enemy retreated. Our young recruits had had their first real contact with the enemy, and not only Roeder, but all the others who had joined us before, had aged years in those final hours. By forcing them to become soldiers and sending them to the front, they had been robbed of their spiritual innocence. They had been forced to die, to sacrifice themselves, to kill. Suddenly life was different, and that part of them - the part that gives eyes a special sparkle in normal life - was extinguished. They had seen the face of war and shaken hands with the devil.

Once again, a number of coils on the trackers' radios ran hot to report the successful defensive battles. On the receivers, too, buttons and switches were fiddled with to send impulses over copper wires to transmission towers. These reports were typed in a secure bunker and sent by telex or verbally over telephone lines to Berlin, the Wolf's Lair or Ober-Salzberg near Berchtesgaden. And while we were lying on hard stone in the dirt and cold, licking our wounds like wild animals and mourning our fallen comrades, somewhere in Berlin or on the Obersalzberg the glasses were raised again to celebrate the partial victory over the enemy. The fine gentlemen drank and boasted of victories won with the blood of the people. Anger arose in me.

The shelling continued. We were sitting on the ridge, the enemy was more or less at our feet. We controlled the roads, but they were constantly shelling us.

In the icy wind and sleet we sat freezing, soaking wet in our holes and eating cold potato soup. Ede sat down and wrote a letter to his wife. I wrote a few lines of this desolation in my diary so that later I could write a letter to my mother in peace. I was looking for beautiful words, for some kind of idyllic landscape to write about, but it didn't exist. I could have written about death, dying, and suffering, but no one at home wanted to read that. No one wanted to know what the mangled corpse of a soldier who had been hit by a grenade while going to the latrine looked like, his body parts scattered in the dirt and excrement around the thunderbolt.

You didn't want to see the tearful faces of the men you had a heroic image of back home. You wanted to see what you hoped to see. Beaming victors in heroic poses. You wanted to see uniforms adorned with regalia and hear the heroic deeds of each of the coveted pieces of metal. They wanted to hear how they had faced down the onrushing enemy and not given them a single yard of space. The reality was different, but no one wanted to know the truth. In my mind, I tried to formulate a letter to reassure my mother.

January 28th, 1944

I couldn't imagine a crueler place than here on the Cassino front. It was cold. Cold as the metal of our weapons. Cold like the stone on which we sat. Cold as the ice on a frozen sea. Cold as the devil's soul.

When I left the barracks less than four weeks ago with some young recruits to march to the front, Thaler and Gebhardt laughed and sang the Westerwald song at the top of their voices. One of them had died miserably because shrapnel had torn open his abdomen, the other had sacrificed a lower leg for the Führer, the people and the fatherland.

Roeder could be back home working as a journeyman in his trade, continuing his education, meeting a girl and starting a family. Instead, he was here at the front, killing attacking British soldiers or hiding from their shells, trembling in fear of death. And as Roeder trembled, so did we all. As he was afraid, so were we all.

After two more repulsed infantry attacks, the Tommy seemed to want to shoot us down. The constant shelling got on our nerves. We crouched down in shell holes or natural depressions. Many were so small that there was room for only one person, in others there were two or three comrades. Almost everyone had chosen a latrine corner where they could relieve themselves during the shelling.

Two comrades from our company went mad. One of them

had a frontal fever and sat in his hole singing. He was taken to the hospital during a break in the shelling. Another jumped out of his cover during an Ari attack and ran like a man possessed through the crumbling shells. He was blown to pieces.

The fate of the soldiers had struck our group again. Wimmer had been killed. A bullet had entered his brain through his right eye. He was killed instantly. Whether it was a stray bullet from an infantryman or a targeted shot from a sniper remained unknown. He lay there as if sleeping peacefully.

The headmaster had done his sad duty and packed the belongings of the fallen. He had sent them to the Spit with their identification tags.

Lieutenant Kohler wrote of their bravery in letters to their families. He awarded all the dead a heroic death and tried to choose words that would make the bereaved proud. Because their sons, husbands or fathers had died for Greater Germany. The families would read the letters and feel immense pain at the sight of their personal belongings. I could relate to that and thought of my brother Robert's grave in Russia.

I heard the rumble of the guns and wondered how many such letters had to be written every day. How many more human victims would the Gustav Line destroy before we retreated and cleared a few hundred kilometers of space. Every day at the front brought suffering to thousands of families. Worldwide.

It had begun to snow. Snowflakes danced in the wind. The canvas tents we had wrapped ourselves in for protection were long since soaked. The moisture was seeping through our uniforms. We were freezing, so it was a relief when the order came to retreat. Detectives crawled from hole to hole, patting the lines. I waited anxiously for one of them to scurry up to my hole.

"Quiet! Pack up, we're being taken out and moved."

"What's the situation?" I asked curiously.

Like the rest of us, the reporter hadn't shaved in days. His hand brushed briefly over his stubbly beard. There were dark circles under his eyes. "There was a real rumble with the 5th Company. Tommy attacked with tanks. But his comrades wouldn't let him break through." Clouds of bre-ath stood in front of the unkempt-looking soldier's mouth.

I stretched my legs and felt exactly as he looked: unkempt, overtired, and exhausted.

"Keep quiet," he repeated. "The retreat should go unnoticed." As soon as he had spoken, the Landser scurried on.

Shivering with cold, I unpacked from the tent and rolled it up. Within minutes I was ready to leave. With chattering teeth I stood and waited. I saw Erwin shouldering his machine gun and was glad I only had to carry a carbine.

The first steps hurt. The thought of the stage, hot soup, warm tea, and heated quarters with a straw bed or even a bed gave me strength.

February 6, 1944

Instead of resting on the stage, we were sent to another part of the front. The battalion had just been transferred from the Monte Natale area to replace the exhausted 44th Infantry Division at Cassino. On this front section of the Gustav Line, American units were pushing hard against our positions in an attempt to break through. Once again, as in Africa, we had to play firefighter to keep the enemy at bay.

A few days earlier, the 36th US Division had suffered a fiasco crossing the Rapido. In foggy conditions, the Texas Rangers set out to cross the raging and flooded Rapido, opposite the village of St. Angelo. Boats capsized as they crossed the river. In the dense morning fog, the men lost their bearings, and those who landed on the other side were caught in a tangle of wire and in the line of fire of the defenders.

The village of St. Angelo, located on a hill, had been largely destroyed by Allied air raids and had since resembled a landscape of ruins. This provided ideal conditions for the construction of the position. Pioneers had also laid minefields and barbed wire in front of the village. The latter were interspersed with booby traps, self-triggering devices for flamethrowers, and some kind of smoke signal transmitter.

After the morning fog lifted, all the German artillery operators had to do was look for the smoke columns to direct the gun fire. The result was devastating. The soldiers of the 36th US Infantry Division lay helpless in the hail of shells. The unit lost nearly 1700 soldiers in a short period of time. They were killed, wounded, or missing.

Several infantrymen lay in the blood and body parts of their comrades, some torn beyond recognition, during the shelling. They experienced and endured horror scenarios. Grenade after grenade fell on their ranks. The detonations drowned out the screams. Shrapnel, dirt, stones, equipment, and even the blood and bones of the fallen were thrown around and poured on the men lying there. They could not move forward or backward.

In addition, German machine gun nests dominated the area, firing belt after belt and ammunition box after ammunition box. The gunners fired at anything that moved.

It was a German sergeant who initiated a cease-fire so that the poor devils could retreat in an orderly fashion and the wounded could be tended to by medics.

(Author's note: Sergeant Josef Jung was awarded the German Cross in Gold for this action and is mentioned by name in the annals of the 36th US Division as Sergeant Joseph Jung).

Example Photo
army-6164896_1920
Pixabay Lizenz: *https://pixabay.com/de/service/license/*

War is cruel and so was the reaction of the US soldiers. After the remnants of the 36th US Division were routed, the 34th US Division attacked with equal ferocity to force a breakthrough in the Liri Valley.

Three infantry regiments concentrated on the high positions, including Mount Maiola, while one regiment advanced toward the town of Cassino. The infantry attacks were preceded by long artillery bombardments.

When we took over the front, our mission was far from simple: we had to retake Monte Maiola. During one of their advances, the Americans had succeeded in throwing our comrades out of their positions and occupying the heights.

Next to us were paratroopers who had been brought in a few days before. They had already joined the battle. Now we were fighting side by side with them against a superior military force, defending every meter of ground.

The Americans fought as tenaciously as the British. Their ammunition seemed inexhaustible, and their artillery got on our nerves.

The enemy was not only numerically superior, but also extremely well supplied and equipped. We found some abandoned winter jackets, which we immediately grabbed to wear under our coats, especially at night. The Americans' cigarettes and canned goods were also a welcome change to our rations. They smoked mainly Lucky Strike. At least a few cartons were left behind. The cans contained mostly meat and vegetable dishes, but there were also some with cookies, sugar or coffee. We were happy to share the unexpected supplies and were curious to see how they would taste.

When you're at the front, you become friends with many of your comrades. My closest friends were my fellow Legionnaires. They had become more like family than ever before.

As we ran toward the heights of Monte Ma-iola at dawn, pushing the American soldiers back over the ridge under heavy fire, Kummerer suddenly collapsed next to me. He looked at me and spat blood. His gaze was blank, but his eyes were not as glassy as Gebhardt's had been lately. I could still see life in them.

"Hang in there," I huffed as I frantically looked around for a medic to help.

Kummerer grabbed my hand, looking for help. He tried to say something, but all he could do was cough up blood. Each red gush was interspersed with many air bubbles. A small trickle had formed at the corner of his mouth and ran down to the collar of his uniform coat. There it was absorbed by the fabric, quickly forming a dark stain.

Lung shot, it went through me.

I returned the weak handshake and felt helpless and paralyzed.

It was Krueger who threw himself on the ground beside us and tore open Kummerer's uniform. To stop the bleeding, he began to apply a bandage with astonishing dexterity. "Straight through. Looks good, old boy," he said in a calm voice. Then he asked for my first aid kit. "Help me!"

I was relieved when a medic ran up at the same moment and

immediately tended to the wounded man. Despite the battle raging around us, the soldier with the Red Cross bandage on his arm radiated something like calm. He spoke to Kummerer in a very routine manner, looked him in the eyes, and checked his pulse. Then the bandage was removed and the wound disinfected. Kummerer sat up.

"That's your house shot for now, comrade. In four weeks you'll be walking through the Black Forest whistling a song," the medic smiled as he tended to his wound.

Two porters had followed him. They waited for the bandage to be reapplied, then grabbed Kummerer and lifted him onto the stretcher. Blood was dripping from his mouth again. Krueger wiped it away with a handkerchief. "When this is over, we'll come and see you."

They left.

I felt a lump in my throat and wanted to cry. I hated war more and more. I hated fighting and I hated the front. There was nothing human left here on the Gustav Line. The last breath of humanity came from the Samaritans of the field: the medics on both sides. At the risk of their own lives, they weaved their way through the ripping grenades and machine-gun fire to rescue the wounded and save lives.

My friend Alfred Kummerer, the butcher from the Palatinate, with whom I had served as a legionnaire in Africa and then in the German Africa Corps, was shot through the lung and sent to the field hospital.

It was done. Once again, at the cost of blood, we had succeeded in driving the Americans from their positions. Now we were on top of a mountain again. The Liri Valley stretched below us. We had a clear view of the small town of Cassino. The Benedictine Monastery of Monte Cassino, founded in the 6th century, was enthroned on the mountain of the same name to our right.

The enemy remained stubborn and continued to press against the front. He constantly covered us with his artillery. The sound and explosion of the shells never seemed to stop. Sometimes it banged directly in our positions, sometimes on one of the neighboring hills, and sometimes down in the town. It was never quiet. The enemy's supply of ammunition and number of guns seemed endless.

When the Allied infantry attacked, our Ari began to cover the area. When our Nebelwerfer batteries took the enemy under fire, the howling of the explosives was reminiscent of the screeching sirens of Stuka dive-bombers and was pure psychological stress for the Allies.

In addition to the American soldiers, the weather was also hostile. It was still very cold. The captured winter jackets were of good quality and kept us warm. I was glad to get one.

When the clouds parted, we were able to observe the attacks of the US troops in the town of Cassino from our positions. We were forced to stand by and watch as our comrades defended themselves against an overwhelming enemy and fought back fiercely.

Last night, in his search for victims, the Grim Reaper tore another Legionnaire from our midst. We lost Willi Faber, the smallpox face. The boy from Hamburg was still joking with Ede, laughing gleefully at a successful joke and putting a cigarette in his mouth. On his way back to his cover hole, a rushing grenade tore him to pieces. Our group had shrunk to six men after Pocke's death. Ede had aged years that night. Anger and despair were eating away at him.

The shelling had intensified again and continued for two more days, with only a few breaks in the fire. There was rumbling and crashing everywhere. Those who could stayed in their hiding places. It seemed as if the Americans were going to shoot us down and take revenge for the loss of the Texas Ranger Division.

Infantry attacks followed. Many of them were stopped by our fierce defensive fire, especially from the tactically ideal machine gun nests and grenade launchers, before they could get dangerously close to the positions.

The Americans were able to overcome this hurdle once. Before daybreak they had bypassed the bullet holes unnoticed. One of our guards noticed them just in time and raised the alarm.

At dawn we saw the figures crawling across the bare rock and opened fire. Erwin hammered away at the attackers with his machine gun. The belt went smoothly and bullet after bullet left the barrel with deadly force. Every seventh round was a tracer, and as he swung the weapon back and forth, the moon face conjured a fine spiderweb of glowing threads across the landscape, at the end of which sat death.

The attacking American unit was stubborn. Despite the fierce defensive fire, they did not retreat. They probably thought their chances of capturing the high ground we held were better than ever. Hand grenades flew back and forth, exploding with a crash. Splinters swirled around. Rifle fire boomed and echoed off the mountain walls. I was loading a new clip into my carbine when I heard a loud roar on my left flank.

US soldiers had entered the position in platoons. All I could hear was banging. Orders were being shouted. A squad jumped up and ran towards the enemy. Erwin rolled around, brought the

MG 42 into position and fired several rounds into the group of approaching American soldiers. He tore a few holes in their ranks and caused total confusion.

Example Photo
war-1172111_1920
Pixabay Lizenz: *https://pixabay.com/de/service/license/*

"Attaaaaack," I heard Ede's rough voice.

Buchecker and Krueger got up and followed him. Erwin and Roeder were now firing again at the Americans, who were fighting their way up the slope in front of us. I didn't know what to do and cursed loudly. Then I jumped up and followed Ede and the others. Out of fear and also to vent my despair, I shouted loudly: "Hurraaaa!"

Another fifty meters, another forty meters, another twenty meters. I was panting. The fast running was exhausting. My lungs went up and down quickly. I thought I could hear my heartbeat and stopped. They ran toward us, mouths agape. I raised the carbine, took aim and fired. One GI fell to the ground. The crowd of men dispersed. The wave had reached us. Our field gray merged with the olive green of the Americans. Close combat. After each shot, I fired as fast as I could, emptying my magazine. Then I dropped the rifle, reached to the side and picked up the folding spade.

Buchecker jumped forward, stretched out both arms, and buried two U.S. soldiers under him. Krueger whirled around with the butt of his carbine as if he were wielding a morning star like a knight. Ede emptied the magazine of his submachine gun with several bursts. An American fired at him. He was standing right in front of me, and I smashed my spade into his shoulder blade. The area immediately turned dark red. The GI dropped his weapon with a scream of pain. At the same time, I felt a hard blow to my back, staggered, barely managed to avoid falling, and instinctively turned around. A US soldier had rammed the butt of his automatic rifle into my back. He swung another blow, which I dodged with a quick step to the right. At the same time, I jerked the spade up with all my might and struck him in the forearm with the sharp edge. He opened his eyes wide and shouted something unintelligible. Before I could strike another blow, he had jumped at me, grabbed me by the collar, and pushed me to the ground. The blow was hard and painful. I screamed. His hands were wrapped around my neck. Memories flashed back. The face of young Tommy from Africa flashed through my mind.

Fight back, it flashed through me.

I tried to breathe, but the pressure on my neck was too strong. I still held the spade with my right hand and took a swing. The blade struck the back of the GI lying on top of me. His face contorted in pain and his grip remained firm. Black spots danced in front of my eyes. In agony, I struck the sharpened edge of the spade two more times against my opponent's back. My face contorted in pain, the American's grip loosened. Quickly, I struck his arms with my free hand and slipped sideways. I was free and gasping for air. My opponent rolled over as well. He had fumbled around on his side with one hand and pulled out a knife. My right fist was still gripping the handle of the spade. When I felt a stabbing movement in my direction, I brought the spade down on the knife hand with full force. The sharpened edge struck my thumb. The knife and the tip of the thumb fell to the ground. The American stared at the exposed bone. I struck a second time and the blade landed in the man's face. A gaping gash stretched across his cheek and chin. Blood spurted out and covered everything. The GI roared and jumped to his feet. His eyes expressed hatred. Before I could strike another blow, he was on top of me again. His fists were pounding on me.

First I saw a shadow above me, then the butt of a pistol, and in a split second, a muzzle flash. The US soldier fell sideways. The shooter had moved on. I only registered that it was an officer, but I couldn't tell who. My eyes fell on the dead U.S. soldier. There was a gaping hole in his head.

Blood seeped out. Instinctively, I grabbed the spade and stood up. I had survived. I had once again cheated death. My mouth opened to scream. The choking caused my voice to fail at first, then I croaked out: "Hurraaaaaaa!"

I ran like a madman, saw an olive green uniform, took a swing, and once again swung the spade into the back of a fighting American soldier. As he turned to face me, the butt of Kruger's carbine struck him in the face. He collapsed. The wound on his back was bleeding and his face immediately swelled up. Blood was also gushing from his nose. The wounded man's right hand lifted. He gave up. Krueger had already struck, but did not land the next blow.

"Thanks, that was close," the father of the Krueger family panted to me.

Ede had inserted a new bar magazine and fired a few rounds. Then his MP 40 fell silent.

The fighting was visibly coming to an end. The enemy retreated.

"Hurraaaa!" could be heard from several sides.

We had managed to repel the invasion of our positions. I sat down almost apathetically. My mind was blank, I couldn't think straight. I dropped the spade and gently massaged my neck. I knew something had to change.

A few minutes later Ede joined me. Miraculously, we had no casualties in our group. And except for a few bruises and scratches on everyone, there were no casualties.

February 11th, 1944

The American units opposite us were pulled out of the front line after days of fighting and heavy casualties. They had fought hard and narrowly missed their objective. Some of their companies had been reduced to squads. The retreat was painful for them, as they had left a heavy toll of blood on the battlefield and achieved nothing.

We also suffered heavy losses, but we were able to hold the front. Like our company, the fighting strength of the other units had been reduced by nearly 75%. A retreat from the front was long overdue. In several companies, sergeants had already taken command of the platoons because the officers had been killed. At the same time, lance corporals were being used as squad leaders.

Our company commander, Captain Geller, had also been wounded in an artillery attack and was in the field hospital. His command post had taken a direct hit. Lieutenant Kohler was put in charge of our company in his stead.

After the fiercest defensive battles, the Cassino front had degenerated into a trench warfare. It was still cold and raining. We were at the end of our tether and expected the enemy to break through at any moment.

As the American troops retreated, their guns also rested. Our supplies took advantage of the lull in the fire and we got a hot meal for the first time in days. A few comrades lined up to see the medic for treatment of minor wounds.

At the food counter I met the sniper who had accompanied

us on the raid the other day and sat down with him. His wound over his eye had been sewn up and a thick layer of iodine tincture had been applied. He had put on bandages to prevent dirt from getting into the wound. Without further ado, I asked if and how he had been used in the last few days. I was very curious and eager to hear what the soldier would tell me. His answer was not what I expected. It was dry and sobering.

"I took turns lying in my prepared positions and shooting at American soldiers. It went better than I thought," he said, pointing to the mangled eyebrow. "It looked worse than it was."

What else was he supposed to do but shoot? I wondered at my own stupid question, thought about it for a moment and added. "And that doesn't haunt you?"

He stopped spooning his goulash out of the cooking pot and looked at me, scrutinizing me. "When the Americans broke in, did you have to go into hand-to-hand combat?"

I nodded.

"You fought, killed and survived. So you know how I feel after every shot."

I shrugged. "I don't understand."

He searched for other words to explain it to me. "Every one of them who ran into my optics could not turn their rifle against you after I shot them, could not ram their knife into your body, and could not smash your skull with the butt of their rifle. I saved your life and the lives of other comrades before that." As soon as he finished speaking, he resumed eating.

From that moment on, I saw the war through his eyes. Every soldier he wounds or kills cannot hurt or kill any more of my comrades, it went through my head. He had developed his own philosophy. Now I knew what I had to do. I would find a sniper training course. "What's your name?"

The sniper shoved a filled spoon into his mouth, chewed a few times and swallowed. "Just call me Toni."

I held out my hand. "Yup."

He didn't take it, but he gave me a smile. It was the first

human trait I had noticed in him.

"Let's eat while it's still warm."

While the 4th Indian Division was still disengaging the American forces to move against the Gustav Line, we finally got our orders to move out. Only the III/361 stayed behind in Cassino City to provide security.

As we gathered, Ede said, sobered and visibly relieved: "Two more days in the hail of Allied guns and the attacks of their infantry and the 7th/361 would have ceased to exist. The order to retreat came at the very last minute. Men, I hope we can recover and regain our strength".

We had faced an overwhelming enemy and were able to repel them despite their material superiority. Our colonel was mentioned by name in the Wehrmacht report and we were finally removed from the front line. We were replaced by paratroopers who had moved up.

When we arrived at the trucks, another disaster awaited us. Our vehicles had been badly damaged by enemy artillery shells. Some of them were so badly shot up that they were unroadworthy.

Improvisation was the order of the day, and in Krueger we had the right man in our ranks. The lance corporal had spent a good hour talking to people from the repair squad and then left. When he returned a few hours later, he was pulling a cart behind him. It was full of spare parts and, to our great astonishment, a cow was trotting along behind it. Krueger had tied it to the wagon with a string.

"I think I'm crazy," said Ede. He pointed at Krueger and couldn't keep his mouth shut in amazement.

"Damn it, Krueger, you have to tie the cattle to the wagon," Erwin yelled at him, joking: "The cattle always go first."

Everyone laughed. This was followed by appreciative slaps

on the back and words of praise for our comrade.

Krueger reported that the Italians here had absolutely nothing to eat and were as poor as church mice. When asked where the beef came from, he evaded the question and simply said: "I didn't rob the Italians. It could be that a supply company's herd has become smaller. Sometimes the cattle just run away and get lost. But I won't say more than that."

We missed Kummerer, our butcher, who would have slaughtered and prepared the animal for us, but Krueger had taken care of that too. He had contacted the butcher company and persuaded one of their butchers to slaughter the animal for us. It was then prepared in the field kitchen and everyone involved in the operation got something to eat.

At first I had my doubts about whether such a thing could be done in total secrecy. But there was so much chaos and confusion that no one really noticed. Properly fed and housed in a heated tent, we felt more comfortable that night than we had in a long time.

The next day we attended a memorial service for the fallen. A field chaplain spoke of God and paradise. I wished I could believe all that, but at the front you are closer to hell than heaven. And during the hours of shelling, I often wondered whose side God was on in this war. On ours or on the enemy's? And if we killed each other, which of us would He let into paradise and which of us would have to go to hell?

I thought of Thaler, Pocke and Gebhardt and came to the conclusion that God does not exist. No God, to whom so much power is attributed, would tolerate such madness.

February 13th, 1944

The vehicles had been repaired to the point where we could get in and move. The picture we presented spoke for itself. The trucks were dented, riddled with bullet holes, and where tarpaulins still hung over the bed, some of them were badly torn. The rear window of our Opel Blitz was missing. The windshield had a crack in the upper right corner, but this did not affect the driver's view.

We looked like a defeated army, and yet we were not helpless on the ground. The rumble of heavy guns could be heard behind us. Soldiers from various nations had joined forces to storm the mountain range we had occupied.

How many nations do you think there are? British, Indians, Americans, Australians, New Zealanders?

I shook the question out of my head and sat back. I was glad to get out of this place. They said we would be transferred to the Adriatic. Even if it was too cold to swim in the sea, the sea air and the silence would mean relaxation for all of us.

Parts of the battalion had already been on the move for hours, and our company was the next unit to leave. Since Ede's Kübelwagen was completely destroyed and nothing more than a pile of scrap metal, he threw his luggage into the back of our Opel Blitz and sat in the passenger seat. "We made it, men. We're going on stage."

We were the survivors of an unequal struggle. I looked at the principal. Like all of us, he was clean-shaven. His uniform was clean and washed. As I had noticed after Pocke's death, the last two weeks had left their mark on him. Ede had become calmer and his hair grayer. None of us were the same as before those days of drumfire, defensive fighting, shock troops, and hand-to-hand combat.

A gendarme whirled around with his fist over his head. The engines were started. After two heavy coughs, our truck started as well.

Ede turned to us briefly. "Are we complete?"

I was about to confirm when I noticed how quiet it was. The man who often provided the entertainment was missing. Krueger.

I was about to tell Ede when Erwin said: "Comrade Krueger is leaving. It won't be long now."

I looked at the moon face. He winked at me.

The convoy started to move while we were still waiting with the engine running.

"Did he freeze on the thunderbeam?" Ede asked. The sergeant got a little nervous: "If he's not there in two minutes, we're leaving!"

Krueger appeared at the same moment. With brisk steps and a bright red head, he came running up, carefully placed his bulging haversack on the back and climbed up. There were beads of sweat on his forehead. He was panting like he had just run a marathon. "Man, that was close."

"Full complement, Sergeant," I called humorously to Ede.

He grinned, bobbed his head slightly, and said to the driver: "Let's go!"

Krueger wouldn't be Krueger if he didn't have a story to tell.

"Guys, I've made a big haul this time," he boasted, opening his haversack. Four unlabeled bottles appeared. "There's homemade grappa in there. Someone from the battalion office organized it. The guy's the Ia's right-hand man."

Erwin grabbed one of the bottles and pulled out the cork. Then he held the bottle up to his nose and smelled it. "If this stuff is good for the chief of staff, it's good for us. I hope it tastes as good as it smells."

A voice came from the front: "You're on duty, comrades. If you start drinking, you'll be marching to the Adriatic on foot."

The cork went back in, and it squeaked a little as Erwin pressed it in firmly. "Don't worry. It's too early for me, too."

We were curious. "Come on, tell me," I nudged Krueger, who had sat down next to me. "How did you get this stuff?"

The lance corporal leaned back. "Actually, I just wanted to say goodbye to my buddy in the field kitchen. As I passed the hospital tent, I saw that a small line had formed. Holiday returnees who had visited a brothel at their last stop and picked up sack rats or something worse. Anyway, I got in line too, and when it was my turn and the pa-ramedic told me to drop my pants, I just said that I had the same illness as the others, but also extreme diarrhea. I danced back and forth, grimaced and said, "It's starting again.

We laughed out loud.

"He put an ointment in my hand and said it would burn. Then he sent me away.

Some held their stomachs and couldn't catch themselves. "You're a hell of a guy."

"And why did you do that?" Elmar Roeder wanted to know. "Do you have any pocket rats?"

Krueger cleared his throat. "Listen, boy. Of course not!" He raised his hands as if to dismiss the insinuation. "Organizing is like playing chess," he explained. "You always have to think two or three moves ahead."

"Go on," Erwin urged.

Krueger didn't need to be asked twice. "I took the ointment to the field kitchen. My buddy Fritz Lochner is a great cook, but also a real rascal. I knew he wouldn't give up any of his black stocks voluntarily. Then I had an idea. I knew he'd had some kind of liaison with at least two nurses, and I casually mentioned that I'd overheard a conversation about nurses and sexually transmitted diseases in the military hospital.

Krueger paused for a moment. Then he pointed to his face. "Guys, you can't imagine how white Fritz became."

We laughed. Krueger was in his element and grimaced at his comments.

"I showed the kitchen-bull my ointment and said it was a real miracle cure for this venereal disease. Then I put it on and said goodbye." He slapped his thighs with the flat of his hand and laughed out loud. "You should have seen the look on his face. Fritz came running after me, tapped me on the shoulder and asked if I knew the names of the nurses. I said no and realized I had him on the hook. By the end of the conversation, the ointment was in his pants pocket and the four bottles of schnapps he had just snatched from the Ia's desk mate were in my knapsack".

Krueger leaned back proudly.

"You can't run into him so fast," Roeder warned.

"At least he has an ointment in reserve," grinned Krueger.

Our progress was slow. This was mainly due to the fact that we had to make way and move to the side of the road to clear the way for supply vehicles to move forward.

After the military police had warned us of low-flying aircraft, Erwin was ordered to provide air defense with his machine gun. "That's not anti-aircraft fire, but I'll give them a run for their money if they attack us," the moon face replied.

Below Rome, some drivers reported problems with their vehicles. In addition, fuel was once again extremely scarce. Our engine went on strike as well, and in the end the whole company had to wait a whole day for repairs and a load of fuel before they could continue on a makeshift basis.

That same day, we heard the news that the Allied bomber fleets on the Cassino front had reduced the city and the Benedictine monastery of Monte Cassino to rubble.

This report made us feel queasy. According to the reports, it must have been a gigantic bombing raid. Nearly 200 Allied bombers, divided into two attack waves, darkened the sky, unloaded their deadly cargo over their target area, and made the monastery mountain tremble.

Just a few days before, we had been in position near the monastery and, together with the III/361, units of our division were also in the town of Cassino.

The thousand-year history of the monumental building was destroyed in a single day. Walls several meters thick crumbled under the hail of tons of bombs, burying monks and civilians seeking shelter.

After the last wave, enemy artillery struck again, plowing over the rubble.

Not a single German soldier was inside the monastery at this time.

After the attack, the surviving monks and civilians were evacuated by evening. German paratroopers then occupied the ruins. The ruins of the destroyed monastery provided not only sufficient cover, but better cover than before the devastating bombardment.

February 16th, 1944

At first they were just small dark dots in the sky. As the silhouettes grew larger, they were accompanied by a low hum that steadily increased. A warning cry rang through my body.

"Air raid!"

The hope that it was German fighters circling in the air was quickly dashed. They were not Focke Wulf or Messerschmidt planes, but American P-51 Mustangs.

The drivers stepped on the accelerator in search of cover. The road we were on meandered through a sparsely vegetated area. There were no extensive hardwood forests to take cover. There was nothing but a ditch and the dusty road itself.

We clung to the wooden benches so tightly that the whiteness of our ankles was visible. Fear crept up and coursed through my body.

"Bloody hell!" Erwin grumbled loudly. "How am I supposed to shoot at the planes if you drive like a hangman?"

The low hum of the engines had grown to a roaring roar. There were five of them. They had lowered their noses and began to dive. Muzzle flashes flashed from the wings. The misses from the weapons on board could be seen through small fountains of dirt and rocks splashing along the dusty road. The hits on the truck's sheet metal sounded cold and tinny.

Wrrrummm ... rrrt ... rrrt ... wrrrummm

They raced across us in rows. The shadows of their wings flitted over the vehicles in the convoy like giant birds of prey.

"Pull over!" Ede squealed as loud as he could as he was thrown up and down in the passenger seat.

Our driver pulled out of the convoy and braked hard. Meanwhile, the pack of fighters had flown a loop, regrouped, and attacked a second time. The Opel Blitz came to a stop. The driver and passenger doors flew open. We jumped out of the back. Erwin rolled once around his own axis with his MG 42 pressed close to his chest. As soon as he came to a stop, he jumped up, ran to the hood of the truck and lowered the bipod of the machine gun. The barrel of his weapon was pointing up.

The Mustangs buzzed overhead like birds of prey. The noise of their propeller engines drowned out the rattle of the on-board machine guns.

Wrrrummm ... rrrt ... wrrrummm ... rrrt

The bullets hit the trucks hard and dry.

Clack ... clack

Erwin had remained calm. He aimed and pulled the trigger. The moon face emptied the entire belt drum. Then he roared loudly and punched his chest with his right fist. "Yaaaaaay ... I scored a hit!"

The planes spiraled upwards again. One of them left a small black cloud behind. None of us could confirm whether the hit or hits had actually come from Erwin's machine gun. He claimed it anyway, and we patted him on the back for it.

As quickly as the attack had come, it was over. Our company suffered three wounded, two dead, one completely destroyed and two damaged vehicles.

The rest of the way to the Adriatic Sea we covered in the dark near Pescara.

February 18th, 1944

It was good to lie on a bed of straw in the dry at night, knowing that the front was miles away. You could stand it on the stage. After breakfast, weapons maintenance was on the schedule. You could go to the doctor, dentist or barber, and everyone waited anxiously for the new arrivals. In the morning, supplies arrived from home.

"Fresh blood for the front," said Krueger.

They arrived at noon. Only 18 years old, barely a beard, and the uniforms were ill-fitting. I had the impression that the boys had been recruited straight out of school and put into a uniform that was far too big for them. They were even younger than the group that had arrived with me.

"They wouldn't have lasted a week in the Legion," Erwin whispered.

We took three of the very young recruits into our group.

Hassmann, Gaensler and Kraus. According to them, they were only in their fourth month in the Wehrmacht. After an abbreviated basic training, they had been transferred to various field replacement battalions for a period of three weeks before being sent to the front.

"I'm going to puke," Ede complained, unbeknownst to the recruits. "They're kids. How the hell am I supposed to work with them at the front or lead a raid? I have to make sure they don't get lost!"

In addition to the three very young recruits, a midshipman was introduced to us as Lieutenant Kohler's replacement. The officer candidate was supposed to be the assistant platoon leader, but our lieutenant had vacated the platoon leader position by moving up to company commander. Kohler said that in Ede Schwarz he had the best platoon leader in the company and that it would be a good fit.

The ensign was a likeable young man who, for his age, already had good opinions and a good leadership style. To me, he embodied the new generation of officers. Still, he had a lot to learn and was more of a liability than an asset in the eyes of the older officers. He was only a recruit of a special rank.

For the recruits, troop training began immediately upon enlistment, and the officer candidate was a part of it. He was willing to do anything, which earned him a lot of respect. His name was Theo Zech and he was from Wiesbaden.

Krueger was to teach the boys as much as possible. The focus was on weapon handling and field behavior, as well as recognizing, executing, and giving tactical signals. The ensign never left the old corporal's side during the exercises.

At the same time, it was announced that a shortened sniper course would be offered. Participants were to find other good marksmen in the company and train them as snipers.

"That's a joke," Ede laughed smugly and made a disparaging gesture with his hand. "There are usually training companies for that, and the courses last anywhere from four weeks in an emergency to three months on a regular basis. In four days, you just learn how to handle a gun, calculate distances, and maybe one or two pointers on how to proceed. It's madness."

In a way, the Schoolmaster was denouncing Germany's helplessness. We had been bleeding on all the world's fronts since 1939 and were in constant retreat everywhere. It was an unspoken secret that the war was lost. Nevertheless, this sniper course was on my mind. I had every interest in attending. Ever since my first encounter with the sniper in the shock troop, I had been tempted to become one of them. I would rather have the distance to the enemy than face them in close combat.

"...and then they expect me to volunteer," Ede finished the sentence.

"I'll go with you."

Stunned looks. The sergeant scratched his head and looked at me. "Jupp Altmann, do you really want to hold a sniper rifle?"

"Yes," I said confidently. "And I want to save the lives of my comrades first," I tried to explain using Toni's words.

February 19th, 1944

The first day of the abbreviated sniper course was theory. We sat in a large tent that had been converted into a training room. The first sergeant leading the course was a sniper himself, a veteran of the Eastern Front. A black patch over his right eye was probably the reason he was standing in front of us in this improvised training room, instead of lying down at the front and aiming at the enemy through a telescopic sight. His left eye was a steely blue and his gaze was penetrating. The big tent was set up. The first sergeant sat at the front. Next to him on a table was a K 98 with a telescopic sight, binoculars with auxiliary sights, various ammunition, tools and maintenance equipment for the telescopic sight, cleaning equipment for the weapon, a combat knife, a compass, a cover mirror and a cover for the camouflage helmet. A camouflage slip jacket, also known as a sniper jacket, and a camouflage patterned tent rounded out the equipment.

As soon as we entered the tent, each of us stared at the equipment with interest. There were twenty of us, and except for Ede, we were all team rank. When the last seat was taken, the first sergeant stood up. A few comrades who had been talking animatedly fell silent.

"Has everyone signed the list?" The voice was rough, dark and commanding.

They nodded. Some answered indistinctly: "Yes."

Without elaborating, the instructor began: "I am Master Sergeant Johannes Zapf. I was a sniper in the 6th Army at Stalingrad. Shortly before the kettle closed, I lost my right eye in a fight with Russian snipers. After I recovered, the 6th Army no longer existed."

We listened to the sonorous voice. He had us spellbound from the first sentence. Without further ado, he explained that this course had nothing to do with sniper training, but that it was better than nothing. What followed were the shortest and most interesting hours I have ever experienced in the military.

The master sergeant interwoven the explanation of the equipment with real-life missions, pointing out the importance of each item and its area of application. Patience and camouflage, for example, were just as important as the right shot, calculating the distance, and choosing the right ammunition when it was available and could be selected.

He hammered three questions into our heads: How do I get into my position undetected, how do I get out, and where is my next change position?

A short instructional movie followed. Then the use of the rifle scope was explained and possible aiming errors were pointed out. As far as rifles were concerned, the Karabiner 98 was still the preferred weapon as it was superior to the modern rifle 43 in terms of range and accuracy.

He moved from the rifle to the ammunition, holding up the

appropriate cartridges as he explained. "As the name suggests, hits can be observed with the Observation Cartridge. Upon impact, both a small flame and a small cloud of smoke can be seen. Behind a phosphorus charge is a capsule containing lead azide or nitropenta."

The next incendiary projectile was shown with the Pr cartridge, where Pr stands for phosphorus. At the end of the various cartridges, the Russian veteran mentioned the steel-core projectiles and also explained the use of tracer ammunition.

The day came to an end very quickly, and in the evening we sat together with the compatriots of our platoon over a glass of red wine and celebrated Mondgeicht's promotion to lance corporal. The mute and I received our corporal's chevrons. There were also plans to send Krueger to an NCO course.

For a few hours, the hardships of the front were forgotten. I would have liked to have another glass or two of wine, but Ede and I decided against it because of the field training scheduled for the next day.

Our three new recruits and the young ensign were also present at the ceremony. But Krueger had honed them so well in the field that all four retired early and went to sleep.

"They're good boys," he said. "My big one will be ready in two years. I just hope the war is over by then," he added. His eyes were pensive and worried. You could tell that his thoughts were at home with his family.

Erwin sensed that he was feeling a little melancholy and stood up. His cheeks glowed fiery red, living up to his nickname. "Raise your glasses! To us, to the wounded, and to our fallen comrades!"

"Cheers!" came from many mouths.

Erwin's voice was heard again. "A song!"

As soon as he asked us to sing, he sang probably the most famous German pop song of that time: "Vor der Kaserne, vor dem großen Tor ...".

We joined in: "... steht eine Laterne ..."

February 20th, 1944

The rainy weather had cleared and the sun was rising over the Adriatic. It was cold. The damp grass crunched under each step. The morning dew glistened in the sunlight and looked frosty in the shade.

The armorer had rolled up in a two-horse carriage. He had everything we needed on the back. The equipment was distributed in an orderly fashion. First we received camouflage jackets, nets for the helmets, binoculars and combat knives. After everyone was equipped, we continued with the weapons. Each shooter was given a K 98k with a 41 scope mounted on it and an 08 pistol with two magazines. In addition, 50 rounds were distributed for the rifle and 32 rounds for the 08. After a short but intensive briefing we received a bag for the ZF 41 *(Rifle scope)* including tools.

On a makeshift shooting range, we learned how to shoot with a scope. We had to estimate distances, recognize camouflaged targets and adjust the weapons to the weather and light conditions. The first sergeant also showed us different types of aiming. He instructed us to use aids such as branch forks. This was followed by exercises in the adjacent terrain. I soaked up every tip, every comment, no matter how small, and every piece of advice. I knew that the only way I could survive in the field was to be careful, not get spotted, and have options for retreat.

"Normally, each sniper works with an observer. We don't have time to practice that with you. But you should have heard it at least once. If you have the opportunity to go out in pairs, take advantage of it. Four eyes see more than two. You'll be more effective and your own protection will increase.

February 21, 1944

On the third day of the course, we repeated the exercises of the previous day, with the Sergeant Major emphasizing the 3-W rule and the development of camouflaged positions. "You can all shoot, we saw that yesterday. Otherwise, you wouldn't have been sent on this course. The important thing is that you come out of the position in good shape after you shoot," he said, pointing to his eye patch with his index finger. "I was a tenth of a second too slow, otherwise I would have come out unscathed. If I had taken a tenth of a second longer, the Russian's bullet would probably have hit me right in the forehead. So much for time. After the shot, you have none! In Stalingrad, the Russians often worked with several snipers. They hunted us by setting traps. One played the hare, the others were the hunters. They were successful. That's all I want to say." He put his index finger down again.

We stood in a semicircle around the Stalingrad veteran. He reached into his pocket and pulled out a pistol bullet. "Snipers are feared and hated. In Russia the hatred was extreme and the war colder and crueler than here."

I listened, wondering if the cruelty of what I had experienced could be surpassed.

"I have always kept this bullet for myself. You're not allowed to say it officially, but I still stand by it: Before Ivan captured me, I would have put it through my head."

At first there was a murmur, then silence. An oppressive silence. We waited for an explanation, and we got one.

"One of our comrades was missing. We found him three days later during a counterattack. The Ivan had captured him and recognized him as a sniper. His death must have been premature. Among other things, they had rammed the barrel of his rifle into his backside. Besides, the corpse no longer looked like a man.

The instructor's expression was cold. There was a frightening gleam in the sergeant's healthy eye as he indicated a cut-like movement at the level of his genitals.

"They cut off his balls and stuffed them in his mouth. His arms and legs were broken." Short pause. "Now you know why I always carried that one bullet with me."

There was a murmur.

"My advice is this: if you are threatened with capture, comrades, get rid of your weapons and anything else that might indicate a sniper. If that's not possible, think about how you want to die."

One of the men murmured: "What you're saying is..."

He didn't get any further. In a flash, the sergeant stood nose-to-nose with the corporal. "What do I mean?"

The corporal stammered out the sentence rather than pronouncing it fluently. "A German soldier does not kill himself. He fights for his Führer *(Leader = Adolf Hitler)*, his people and his fatherland until..."

The master sergeant interrupted: "... until the enemy cuts off his balls or rams a rifle barrel up his ass. Shall I take a picture of you like this and send it to your family? I can write on it that you died like a hero..."

"It's all right," Ede interrupted. "Sometimes it's better not to say everything."

The master sergeant took a step back, gave Ede a quick look, and said: "That's enough words for today. Does anyone else have a question or would any of you like to make a comment?"

A general shake of the heads. The private who had scoffed at our instructor's words also shook his head. "No, those were clear and unmistakable words."

The instructor walked over to the table and patted the stock of the 98 karabiner lying there. "See you tomorrow," he said quietly and began to pack the ammunition.

February 22nd, 1944

The fourth day of the short course did not take place. At the front, the enemy was pushing hard against our defensive line, and we got our marching orders that evening. Although the sparrows were already whistling from the rooftops and we had expected something like this, we were worried. Our deployment came sooner than we would have liked. The new recruits were anything but ready for action, and we old warhorses were still battered and bruised.

It was only 30 kilometers to the front and we left that same night. Only a few hours later we took up position in the Pescara-Ortona area. We had barely been briefed and had more or less settled in when the British artillery started firing and covered us with shells for hours.

Huuiiit - wham

There it was again. The clatter of the heavy suitcases. The crashing and exploding, the whirring of shrapnel and the acrid smell of gun smoke.

We felt sorry for the recruits. They were pale, shocked and frightened. We didn't blame them. From our point of view, they were schoolboys and far too young for the front. They were nothing more than cannon fodder whose job it was to die for the Nazi Party bosses. Infused with the ideas of National Socialism, the camaraderie and adventures of the Hitler Youth, they knew no other world. Like me, they succumbed to the charm of the uniform and are paying for it here and now: At the front, in the hail of Allied shells.

Ede and I were considered trained snipers, but only I was supposed to go hunting. Our Schoolmaster was assigned to lead the platoon instead and was therefore indispensable.

While the smaller and larger calibers rattled around us, I crouched in my cover hole and jotted down a few lines for my mother. Kraus and Gaensler, two of the recruits, sat across from me and couldn't get a word out. Kraus tried hard to hide a tremor.

I shoved my notebook and pencil back into my breast pocket and buttoned up. "Who knows when I'll get around to it again," I said to break the silence.

There was no answer.

"We had the same experience in Africa. When we arrived, Tommy greeted us with his guns. You never get used to it, but you learn to live with it," I tried to encourage her. "I almost wet my pants that time," I added, eliciting a slight grin from both of them.

Huuiiit - wham

This time the impact was so close that we instinctively ducked our heads. The detonation sent a trickle of fine earth and stone fragments flying towards us. The smell of the billowy gunpowder vapor stung our lungs. Fortunately, it didn't last long.

It was cold, windy, and light sleet was falling.

We fell silent again and I let my mind wander. A priest had told us that we German soldiers were hated and feared, but also respected. We were not generally considered Nazis, and yet there was a kind of hatred toward us. When we asked the Englishman where this hatred came from, he said that we Krauts were very good soldiers in the eyes of the Allies. We were considered cold and cruel because we fought tenaciously for every inch of ground. We were considered ruthless because we fought back even when we had fired our last bullets. And when the enemy attacked in equal numbers, we always won. So they were forced to attack in superior numbers, which meant high casualties.

Of course, I couldn't confirm any of this, but I couldn't deny it either. We gave the prisoner something to smoke and half a can of *Scho-ka-Cola*. I think we just wanted to show our humanity with this gesture.

When the word humanity crossed my mind, I looked down at my sniper rifle.

Can I remain human if I kill on purpose?

My first mission as a sniper was tomorrow before dawn. It

wasn't the persistent rumble and thunder of the guns, it wasn't the whimpering sounds of the half-asleep recruits, and it wasn't the thunderous impact of the grenades that kept me awake on this icy February night. It was the thought of my mission tomorrow.

February 23rd, 1944

The Allies would not have needed the Gustav Line to stop them or allow them to advance at a snail's pace. The weather took care of that without any help from us. Continuous rain was replaced by light snow showers, only to change back to continuous rain. It was cold. The bad weather front had softened the ground, causing it to freeze and then soften again, turning the terrain into a swampy landscape that was almost impassable for heavy vehicles. Tanks and trucks made very slow progress. Our minefields and barbed wire tangles did the rest.

It was still bitterly cold and I had barely slept. My first sniper mission was clear and simple, but difficult to execute. Allied fire was well directed. Somewhere in the area, one or more forward artillery observers from the Tommies had taken up position. My mission was to move forward with the relief of our outposts before sunrise, observe the terrain from a good position, locate the artillery observers, and eliminate them.

As much as I was impressed by the extremely short training and fascinated by the sniper rifle and its equipment, I cursed it all that night. It was crazy: while all around us the grenades rained down, plowing up the earth and blowing funnels into the bare rock, I remained mostly calm and reassured my new comrades. And now that I was about to do exactly what I thought I could do to escape the hated, conventional infantryman's existence, I was overcome by an oppressive fear that wouldn't go away.

Five men waited at the rendezvous point. Two men each for

the two outpost positions and another Landser. As I approached and recognized his face, a small weight fell from my shoulders. It was Toni, the sniper. Before I could even get a "good morning" out of my mouth, he greeted me with these words: "The old man has assigned me to you. I still can't shoot properly," he pointed to his eye. "There are still dark spots dancing around. But it's good enough for observation. I'm supposed to assist you."

"We're all set," murmured an older corporal with a Swabian dialect. "Follow me and shut up. Tommy likes to send out shock troops to take prisoners."

The Swabian looked familiar: I'd seen him several times before, but I didn't know his name.

"Stay in line behind me and try not to make a sound."

One of his companions was definitely one of the new recruits. His face was milky bearded and his uniform hung on him like a wet sack. It was at least two sizes too big. He lined up right behind the lance corporal. Two privates followed him, then me. Toni was the last man.

There was no sound except the sound of our boots on the mud. Sometimes we sank ankle deep, sometimes the ground beneath us was rocky. At one point there was a strong stench of decomposition.

"There is a body here somewhere. One of our predecessors told me that. It hasn't been found yet in this rough terrain," whispered the corporal in front of me.

The path wound through the dense trees and undergrowth and finally led to a small hill. The corporal stopped. We caught up with him.

"The first picket should be waiting for us here. Stay here, I'll have a look."

He disappeared into the darkness. I looked at my watch but couldn't see anything.

"It'll be dawn in an hour," Toni whispered to me.

A rustling. My hand went to the holster of the pistol. The outline of the lance corporal appeared. "All right. You two can go," he pointed to the two privates.

We walked to the second outpost, approaching it carefully so as not to be mistaken for Tommy's. The corporal shouted the password twice in quick succession. After a short briefing, he and the recruit took over the position. Toni then talked for several minutes with one of the two soldiers. I took the opportunity to relieve myself. When I came out of the bushes, Toni waved to me. We walked on.

After crossing two small hollows and hills, we reached the ideal spot. The trees and bushes were so dense that our camouflage made us hard to spot.

It was cold, wet and very uncomfortable. Like me, Toni had camouflage gear in his backpack, as well as a blanket and tent fly. He also pulled out a sheepskin. "You should get one of these," he said.

It was dawn, and the rising sun offered a good view of the landscape ahead. Toni held his binoculars to his eyes and watched the surrounding terrain. The silence of the rather taciturn man reminded me of the mute man. I wondered what Toni did for a living in civilian life.

He put down his binoculars for a moment and said: "The weather is good for us, they can't send their planes up there."

I looked up. "Yeah, that's right."

The Tommy started spraying the area again with his artillery.

Toni raised the binoculars. "Look for anything that looks suspicious. Something that could be an antenna, a reflection of glass, a flash, a cigarette burn. Whatever, just look for it."

I nodded and began to explore the area with my binoculars. I didn't recognize anything. The constant observation of the landscape made my eyes tired. The cold wind made me shiver and I was glad I had packed my blanket and tent. This was one of the most important tips of the sniper course for me at that moment. The second tip, which I followed to the letter, was to stay under cover. To keep my legs from falling asleep, I alternated between moving my toes, then pulling my knees up and stretching my legs out again. Sometimes both legs together, sometimes each leg separately. Time passed slowly, and conversation didn't seem to be part of the sniper's repertoire. Whenever I tried to start a conversation, the man next to me would shut it down and point to the binoculars: "Keep an eye on the area. We have to find the artillery observers."

Toni didn't seem to mind lying down for so long. As far as I could tell, he had moved maybe two or three times in the last five hours.

I was dog-tired, lying around letting the cold slowly creep through my tent, blanket, and uniform. My eyes closed at shorter and shorter intervals. I was about to put down my binoculars and rub my hands together when my adrenaline level shot up from one second to the next.

"There he is," my neighbor had muttered. "Get your rifle. I've got him!"

Goose bumps covered my back. I fumbled for the rifle and pushed it forward. "Where?"

"Eleven o'clock. Small hill. Small rock outcropping, some ca-rob trees behind it. There are at least two men. One is between the trees in the second row, the other is by the rock. I think the one in the back is the radio operator. The one in front is hard to make out. He is lying under some kind of camouflage net. They have done an excellent job of camouflaging themselves."

I uncovered the optics, searched for the spot described, and put it on. The shaft felt cold. I was wide awake. The fatigue was completely gone. Centimeter by centimeter I searched the described place. Then I recognized a small movement. "I saw the one in front."

Toni spoke without taking off the binoculars. "You have to take out the radio operator first and then the Ari observer with a second shot. He won't leave his position. Conversely, the radio operator will retreat."

Toni thought along with me. I probably would have acted differently. I had learned something again. I searched doggedly for the radio operator, but all I could see was the foliage of the evergreen carob trees. "We were told to fire only one shot from one position," I pointed out.

"If we're facing snipers or fighting infantry, that's the way it is. A second shot would be a sure death sentence. You can't rule out the possibility that the Tommy also has snipers in the area, but then our outposts would be the first to go."

I circled the carob trees several times, but found nothing. "Are you sure the radio operator has taken up position there?"

"No, but that is what I would do."

A little annoyed, I took off again. After another minute I actually had him in sight. That is, I saw the radio operator's knee. It looked like he was sitting cross-legged behind one of the trees. "I have the knee."

"I can see it. That's your target."

"The knee?"

"You're going to take him out with this. If there's a second radio operator, we'll startle him. After the shot, you will aim at the Ari observer and take him out!"

I took a deep breath. The Brit's knee bobbed up and down slightly. I had him in my sights. Pressing the stock of the rifle against my cheek and shoulder, I searched for the pressure point and curled my index finger on the trigger until I felt the first slight resistance. With the barrel resting on the ground, I knew the shot was guaranteed to be on target. I took another deep breath, blew part of it out again, held my breath and squeezed the trigger. The shot cracked. I felt the recoil on my shoulder and saw my target flinch through the scope. Toni confirmed. "Hit! Turn around now!"

I walked to the rocky outcrop with my barrel and scope and saw movement. The shot had startled the artillery observer. I recognized the face. He was young. I guessed he was about my age. Maybe a year or two older.

Damn it! I can see the face.

Even though I knew I would see the target magnified through the optics and that the shooting would be different than an attack, I hesitated. There was a young man whose life would be over in a matter of seconds. I felt revulsion and inhibition. Something inside me was resisting. I did not want to pull the trigger.

Toni sensed my concern. "He's directing artillery fire at our positions! Don't feel sorry for him. He doesn't have it in him," he whispered to me. "He blew up dozens of our comrades."

I still had the artillery observer in my sights. The soldier moved. He was crawling backwards very slowly. I realized I had to act immediately. Pocke appeared in my mind. I had the image of a grenade tearing him apart again. A mixture of rage and coldness spread. My breathing was slow, my hands steady. I pressed the carabiner firmly against my shoulder again. Without thinking, I pulled the trigger. As if an invisible fist had struck, the artilleryman's head was thrown back. The body collapsed.

"Hit!" Toni said in a calm voice and kept the binoculars on the target for a moment. "Now we have to change position."

I swung the barrel of my rifle back toward the British man who had been shot. "And the radio operator?"

"That was a tactical target. They'll get him. They're abandoning the position itself. The nest has been dug."

I felt bad. Instead of feeling the joy of having successfully completed a mission, I was overcome by a feeling of helplessness. I had intentionally seriously injured a person and killed a young man. I felt sick. My stomach tightened and I could feel the chyme trying to move from my stomach up through my esophagus. I swallowed, took a few deep breaths, and managed to fight off the feeling that I was going to throw up.

"We have to go." Toni tapped my shoulder. "It's war. We're soldiers and we're only going to kill people who are going to kill us and our comrades or cause them to be killed."

I waved her off. I didn't want to hear anything. No justifications and no reasons. I saw Pocke's face again, then I remembered Gebhardt's screams. It's all right,' I replied.

Of course, it was anything but fine, but I needed some rest.

The artillery fire was scattered in our front, since the forward observer had been switched off. The shells were no longer aimed, but fired irregularly.

We didn't know if the injured British radio operator had been rescued. I thought I heard the occasional whimper or groan. But maybe my senses were playing tricks on me and it was just the sound of the wind blowing over the land.

We took up position again and stayed there until dusk. Then we retreated completely. Our suspicion that the constant artillery fire was in preparation for an attack was quickly confirmed. During the night the enemy attacked our positions. The battalion was at an allied interface. While three companies were fighting Canadian infantry, our company was fighting a New Zealand unit.

With Toni's assistance, I had prepared three positions the evening after our return so that I could quickly change positions if necessary. I was positioned with my sniper rifle slightly away from the groups and had an almost perfect field of fire. To-ni was my observer. I profited from his experience.

Only a small part of the terrain in front of us was obscured by vegetation. This advantage was used not only by me, but also by our machine-gun nests. The riflemen hammered away at the New Zealand infantrymen with their machine guns. There was crashing, flashing and thundering at every corner. Again and again flares whizzed into the air, illuminating the area for precious seconds. In the shaky, artificial glow of the magnesium light, we searched for the enemy and fired.

The enemy wanted to drive us out of our positions. The Ortona-Pescara road was the second, besides the Via Casilina on the west coast, on which heavy armored vehicles could drive towards Rome. The Allies were therefore forced to break through our lines.

The attack was carried out with full force, and it was probably only due to the bad weather that no heavy armored vehicles were used against us. They would inevitably have gotten stuck in the muddy terrain.

After the enemy had established itself, our company prepared to counterattack. The goal was to take prisoners and push the enemy back.

Our machine guns and the grenade launcher unit took over the barrage.

The tracer ammunition once again stretched across the terrain like a deadly spider's web. The thud of the grenades could not be heard over the continuing din of battle. The whirring sound of the approaching vortex was also drowned out. It was only when the explosives hit and exploded one after the other that there was a huge bang.

Rrrrt.

Wham wham wham

Toni and I followed. It was anything but easy to follow the attacking company in the dark and to fend off possible dangers or ambushes with well-aimed shots. That's why we inevitably got closer to the soldiers and I was glad when I recognized the outline of the mute. The former shepherd cursed softly as he kept sinking his boots deep into the mud, almost losing contact with the group. Pulling the boot out was not so easy. At least if you wanted to keep your feet dry and not slip out of the boot.

The gunfire ahead of us suddenly increased. Muzzles flashed in several places at once. Machine guns rattled. Men were panting, shouts could be heard. As a flare shot up into the sky, casting its halo of light over the area, I realized the men were in hand-to-hand combat. Aimed shots with the rifle were not possible. Toni pulled the .08 from the holster. I slung the rifle over my shoulder and drew my pistol. My heart was racing.

Huge amounts of adrenaline coursed through my bloodstream.

The mute grabbed the spade and with a primal scream swung the sharpened edge at a dark-skinned New Zealander running toward us. The blow was delivered with such force that the attacker's neck was almost completely severed. The soldier's head fell to the side. Blood spurted from the open wound. Someone next to me vomited loudly. I stumbled over the fallen soldier and recognized the face of one of the newcomers in the fading artificial light. It was Hassmann.

I sat up. Toni was on my right and fired a few shots. The flare had burned out. Darkness surrounded us. Muzzle flashes flashed again and again.

"Ahhh ..."

A Maori suddenly stood in front of Toni and rammed a bayonet into his torso. I jerked my right arm up and fired three times in a row. The New Zealander collapsed. Toni went to his knees as well. He dropped the 08 and slumped forward. I was afraid he would sink his face into the muddy, swampy ground and suffocate. Two quick steps and I was there. "Toni," I called, but by the time I grabbed his uniform and turned his body over, he was already dead. Anger and grief mixed. "No! Damn war," I shouted as loud as I could and began to cry. I no longer had the strength to get up and fight. "Cursed war," came whimpering from my lips.

The counterattack was successful and started the retreat of the Allies. Their attack was repulsed all along the front. Toni and Hassmann were killed. Gaensler was wounded in the shoulder. More serious, however, was the shattered right side of his face: a New Zealander had smashed the young soldier's cheekbone and jaw to a pulp with the butt of his rifle.

"Let's hope the doctors patch him up properly," Erwin said. "That didn't look good."

Our party had taken two prisoners. They were Maoris. As they were being taken away, Kruger looked at them and said:

"Not only do they look like that, they fought like savages." Almost admiringly, he added: "I thought I would have to break the skull of the guy who had gone into hand-to-hand combat with me and beat him to death. He just wouldn't give up."

As the sun rose, we sat together in silence. Our eyes were blank. The area had been cleared of the enemy and secured. Medics and soldiers retrieved the bodies. Those of the young recruits who had survived seemed to have aged years. Some of them jumped in fear when a cup fell, others stared impassively. It was as if the front at Monte Casino had robbed the men of their vitality. Barely older than they were, I wondered if the Legion and the Afrika Korps had dulled me to the point where I functioned like a machine, mindless and unfeeling, on command. Could I ever return to a normal life after the war?

February 24th, 1944

Toni had been killed. With his death, I had lost not only my designated observer, but also a good instructor. Despite his taciturnity, I had grown to like him more and more with every hour we spent together. Now he lay in a soldier's grave with many other comrades.

The companies were extremely exsanguinated, the groups decimated and the fighting strength diminished daily. For this reason, the position of observer was not filled. I was immediately left to my own devices as a sniper.

It was still raining cats and dogs and the temperatures were only just above zero. The weather was still as hostile as the Allies.

After the enemy artillery fired only random barrage fire, their infantry units joined in the continuous bombardment and covered us with grenade launcher fire. This meant that we didn't have to deal with the heavy bags of artillery and naval guns, but the rumble was more frequent. The grenade launchers caused us a lot of problems.

Constant shelling, constant shock troops and cold, wet rain tortured us mentally and physically. In addition, the quality of our food had deteriorated considerably. When the food carriers came, the meals were chilled and anything but hot. In cold, wet weather, cold, thin stews don't give you strength. The situation was miserable, and so were we. Miserable, cold, weak and exhausted. I wondered how much longer we could hold out. We were asked to do the impossible and we did it.

The snipers in the companies were always used. At the moment, this special assignment meant that I was with my comrades and was supposed to fight alongside them. Our platoon had been reduced to 19 men. The company itself had lost more than half of its fighting strength. Nevertheless, the orders coming down from the division to the battalions and delegated to us did not stop.

Lieutenant Kohler had called for a briefing. We stood tightly packed around him. The constant rain had soaked the tent roof to the point where water was dripping down on us. This time we were assigned to night patrol.

"The weather is as bad for our enemies as it is for us. The British, Indians, New Zealanders and Canadians are also getting wet. We'll go out, make sure we take a prisoner or two and, at best, find out exactly where some of those damn grenade launchers are. Tomorrow we have a day off for that."

Silence. Except for the pattering rain, nothing could be heard for a brief moment. Ede lit a cigarette. The small flame of the lighter illuminated his furrowed, unshaven face for a moment. A few other Landsers followed Ede's example and also smoked a last cigarette before marching off.

Lieutenant Kohler continued. "Captain Zech leads. Pvt. Altmann will follow a bit behind and provide cover with the sniper rifle. Sergeant Schwarz, select twelve more men."

Ede paused for a few seconds. He wanted to repeat and confirm the order, but Lieutenant Kohler waved him off and added to his order: "You go without the machine gun." He raised his left arm and pulled back his sleeve. A glance at the watch followed. "Prepare to move out. The reconnaissance party will leave in 15 minutes!"

Ede took three strong drags on his cigarette and flicked it aside. The embers went out with a hiss. "You heard the company commander, men. Volunteers first."

All the legionnaires took a step forward. Krueger and Elmar Roeder did the same. The Schoolmaster looked around. Then he tapped Erwin on the shoulder. "You and Roeder stay here with the machine gun." He turned and nodded to some of the other groups. Ten minutes later, seven experienced men and five young comrades were standing there, ready to march. I had noticed that one of the young men was shaking badly, and his neighbor couldn't help but notice.

"Are you all right?" he was asked.

The boy struggled to smile. "It's freezing!"

It was a new moon, it was raining, and it was pitch dark. Our scouting party moved past the outposts into no-man's-land. The ground was soft and muddy. Because of the poor visibility, it was out of the question to accompany the men from the side, so I marched right alongside them. In no time our positions were behind us and we were out in the open. Corporal Gruber from the second squad had taken over the three-man vanguard. He had been out here a few times before and knew the terrain best.

The ground became increasingly soft and muddy. More than once my boots sank up to my ankles in the mud. When I pulled my boots out despite the rain, you could hear the smacking sound as the hole left by the water and mud closed again, followed by a splash as the boot hit the ground and sank back in.

Marching under these conditions was difficult and could not be done in silence. The longer we walked, the more uncomfortable I felt. An alert sentry would have heard that sound, for better or worse. I was expecting to be shot at. My adrenaline level was rising, my pulse was pounding and my heart rate was racing.

I was glad when we turned right and soon came to a narrow road. It was relatively quiet. The rainwater ran into ditches to the left and right of the road. What had been small rivulets had turned into real streams. We followed the road south. After about one kilometer we met Gruber and his two companions. They were waiting for us at a burned out tank wreck. Shell craters covered with debris indicated artillery hits. Pioneers had repaired the road. They had probably used heavy equipment to push the wreckage aside so their tanks could use the road.

Ede spoke briefly with Zech, who ordered the reconnaissance party to move up and stop. They both stood beside Gruber, who reported frantically.

"A mile and a half down the road are some houses that have been shot up. That's where the Tommy has taken up residence. I assume there's a grenade launcher unit there as well."

"We should have hit outposts by now," E-de said.

"Maybe we slipped through a hole," whispered one of Gruber's companions.

"Or the guard is asleep," came a voice from behind.

"Quiet!" warned the schoolmaster. "Corporal Gruber has skillfully led us through the lines. The utmost silence is now in order!"

Gruber cleared his throat: "Or the posts are vacant because of a change. That would be a fatal mistake, but it can happen."

"Change?" asked our officer candidate.

"Yes. We were within a few meters of the ruins and picked up a few scraps of words. It was pure English at first, I'm sure. I know that language very well from Africa. Later it turned into incomprehensible gibberish. I think the Indian troops are just relieving the British or the Canadians.

"Gurkhas?"

There was not only the utmost respect in this one-word question, but also unmistakable fear. Rumors had long circulated in our ranks about these elite Indian soldiers. They were said to be not only excellent with their sharp, curved daggers, but also extremely brutal. They may have been latrine slogans, but there was a kernel of truth in each one. Allegedly, soldiers had been found with their genitals cut off by Gurkhas. I didn't think much of it. The war had long since turned men into wild animals. Anything was possible.

"I'm not sure they're Gurkhas," was muttered.

Another voice answered: "Fuck you! I don't want to get into hand-to-hand combat with them."

"Shut up!" Zech repeated, emphasizing the fact that he had leadership qualities.

We could hear the faint sound of engines. We didn't see any lights. The rain had slowed to a drizzle. Water dripped from the edges of the steel helmets. The uniforms had long since soaked through, and the cold crept through our clothes to our skin.

"They're moving off again," Gruber whispered. "They must have unloaded their cargo!"

Ede thought for a moment, then gave the order: "We go ahead and find out how many men are lying there and if it really is a grenade launcher unit, and also ..."

Noises abruptly silenced the sergeant. The rattling of equipment, a curse and a hissed order in a foreign language could be heard.

"They're sending out a scouting party," Ede whispered, his fingers checking in the dark that the safety on the submachine gun was off.

"Or on their way to occupy or relieve the outposts," Gruber said.

"Spread out! Fire only on my command!" came the logical reply from Zech.

The men scurried aside as quietly as possible. One of them had stumbled over a roll of armor lying around and landed in the ditch with a loud splash.

A split second later, a flare shot into the sky. Trembling,

artificial magnesium light illuminated the surroundings. Some of us had hidden behind the wreckage of the tank, the others crouched in the ditches to the left and right. I had jumped into the ditch as well. Water seeped down the shaft of my right boot. I cursed inwardly. For a split second I hoped I wouldn't catch a cold. What a crazy thought. Here I was, facing the enemy, right in the middle of a firefight, worrying about catching a cold. I took a risk and lifted my head over the edge of the trench. The next few seconds could decide the outcome of the battle.

Hectic shouting could be heard. A group of Indian soldiers were less than thirty meters ahead of us on the road. Their bodies were clearly visible in the light. One of them was waving his hands wildly. He was the one shouting the orders. Muzzle flashes flashed. The bullets hit the wreckage of the tank hard. Ricochets whistled in different directions. At the same time, the enemy scattered. With soldierly automatism, I slid the rifle into position.

"Fire!" I heard Ede's voice.

I took aim at the soldier who kept waving his hands, assuming he was the senior officer or a non-commissioned officer.

When the magnesium light went out, I fired the targeted shot. As if an invisible fist had knocked him down, the soldier jerked his arms back and fell. Then it was dark. The voice could no longer be heard. Instead, there were bangs everywhere. Muzzle flashes could now be seen on both sides. I aimed at the enemy and pulled the trigger. After the shot, I instinctively ducked my head and rolled two turns to the side.

At the height of the ruined houses a second flare was launched into the rainy sky.

Captain Zech gave the order to attack. "Jump up! Attack!"

To the left and right of the trench, Landsers jumped up and charged forward. Two of them fell to the ground. One stayed down, the other stumbled and jumped back up.

Taking advantage of a gap between the enemy and my comrades, I fired another well-aimed shot. Repeating the shot, I also jumped up and ran towards the enemy. "Hur-raaaa!"

A third flare lit up the scene. Close combat. Screams, moans. A machine gun rattled away. The tracer ammunition drew its deadly glowing thread over our heads. Soldiers in platoons ran toward us from the ruins. I emptied my magazine, reloaded, and fired again.

"Retreat!" I heard Ede's voice.

Two Indians raised their hands. Two comrades stood behind them, pressing the barrels of their rifles into their backs. The artificial light flickered and went out.

"The new boss has fallen."

Ede stood like a pillar of salt.

"Sepp Krömer too!" echoed through the night.

The next flares lit up the rainy night eerily, and our outlines were once again targets for the enemy snipers. I knelt down and fired two quick shots at the enemy. They were not even within range of my rifle, but the shots reassured me. After the shots, I repeated myself and ran back to the wrecked tank.

The schoolmaster was kneeling beside Zech, a bullet in his neck and another in his chest. Rainwater washed the blood away toward the ditch.

Krömer lay only two meters away. Someone ripped off his identification tag and ducked as a machine-gun barb whizzed close over him.

Ede took a deep breath. In his mind he wrote the letter to the parents of the young officer candidate. He was brought back to the present by the sound of a machine gun barb spraying small fountains of water close to him. He quickly grabbed the dead man's neck and pulled on the chain of the identification tag. The small metal plate appeared. Ede broke it at the predetermined breaking point and quickly shoved the shard into his breast pocket.

"Retreat!" he repeated loudly and added: "Altmann, Gruber and Krueger, cover the retreat! We have two prisoners."

The group hurried back into the safe darkness of the rainy night, while the three of us took cover near the wreckage and took aim at the enemy. The enemy machine gun stopped firing. Probably they could no longer make out the outlines of our comrades.

"We'll fire twice, then run to the right, fire again, and get out of here as fast as we can," Gruber gushed. "You stay close to me. I'll find the way blind."

"And the others?" gasped Krueger. "Will they find their way, too?"

"My two comrades will lead them."

The Indians, running toward us, came within range. We lined up and fired as agreed. The platoon stopped briefly, seemed to spread out across the terrain, and responded with appropriate return fire.

After our third shot, we jumped up as agreed and hurried after Gruber in a crouching position.

Above us, the wavering magnesium light lit up the sky

again.

"Get down!"

We landed splashing in the mud. We lay in the mud, panting. Our comrades were nowhere in sight. The rain picked up again. The light went out.

"Gruber groaned and jumped up.

Krueger and I ran after him.

We reached our positions completely exhausted, soaked to the skin and frozen to death. Both prisoners were handed over unharmed and taken to the company command post for their first interrogation. You could see the fear in their faces.

Krueger looked at them. "I could have sworn they were trying to escape in the dark."

Ede's reply was cold: "They wouldn't have survived.

I thought for a long time whether the headmaster would have shot them or not. I deliberately didn't ask him. I don't think I could have handled the answer if he had said yes.

What is this war doing to us?

The result of the reconnaissance was bitter. Captain Zech and Sergeant Krömer, a legionnaire from another group, were killed. Three soldiers were wounded. One of them probably saved his life by holding the blade of a Gurkha dagger with his bare hands. They were cut up accordingly. "...and then a big, strong comrade split his skull open with a blow from the butt..." I heard him say and assumed he was talking about the mute.

"Get out of those wet uniforms!"

We didn't need to be told. No one would have lasted more than half an hour in there.

Later we sat together in a small group. A cannon stove was glowing in the crew tent. It had been requisitioned from Canadian supplies, and we were glad to be warm and dry. The mood was subdued. We drank hot coffee and ate biscuits. With the death of the young officer candidate Zech, Ede had been given command of the platoon as the oldest non-commissioned officer.

"Lost another old legionnaire in Krömer," Ede muttered,

pouring some juniper schnapps into his coffee mug. "And a nice young ensign," he added.

Zech's death gnawed at him. I didn't recognize the headmaster at that moment. I realized he was blaming himself.

"Anyone else?" he asked the group, raising the half-empty bottle.

Wordlessly, everyone raised their cups, and the clear liquor brightened the brown broth a bit.

"Let us hope that last night's sacrifices were not in vain," Roeder said.

"Every sacrifice in this damn war is in vain," I slipped out.

But the sentence was drowned out by Ede's simultaneous loud toast: "To our fallen comrades!"

February 26, 1944

We had been in the trenches and foxholes since yesterday morning. Some had built waist-high walls of stones, others of logs or sandbags.

Empty eyes, trembling knees. Three, four, and five-day beards sprouted from the men's faces. Their uniforms were dirty, most of their coats soaked from the rain. The young men stuck to the old men and followed their orders without question. They wanted to survive, and the old men were like guardian angels to them.

I wondered what the difference was between our modern Wehrmacht and the Kaiser's soldiers in the last war. They lay in their trenches at Verdun, soaked in them, got trench foot in the wet, and bled to death in the no-man's-land between their positions and those of the enemy. My original love for uniforms had long since turned to hate. But it wasn't the clothes I hated, it was the people in charge in Berlin, sitting in their wing chairs, smoking cigars and toasting with brandy, while we were out here dying miserably. The fact that we were fighting against the whole world was more evident on no other battlefield in the world than here on the Cassino front: we were already up against the British, the Canadians, the New Zealand Maoris, the Americans, and now the Indians. How were we going to survive? Fear and doubt were written all over my face, as they were on the faces of almost every Landser. Where would we find the strength to withstand any onslaught? We had long since stopped talking about the ideals of the German Reich. We stood up and raised our rifles to protect our lives and those of our comrades. That's how it seemed to me in those weeks. If I had gotten a shot at Hitler or any of the other leaders of the big-mouthed warmongers, I would have pulled the trigger. My hatred grew with every day of suffering and death. It was only a matter of time before it got me.

Example Photo
remembrance-day-2910439_1280
Pixabay Lizenz: *https://pixabay.com/de/service/license/*

"Stay down! Some are swirling again!" they warned.
They were referring to the hated shells of the Allied mortar

units. It was like choosing between the plague and cholera: you could hear the heavy shells whistling from the guns, and every soldier knew he had to keep his head down and take cover. But this quiet whistling often came with a surprise effect. Eventually, the explosives would lower their noses, detonate, and scatter their fragments dangerously.

Wham - wham – wham

Heads were pulled in. It rumbled several times in succession. Shrapnel, mud, stones, and splinters of wood swirled with the pressure waves, smashing against everything in their path. Powdery clouds of smoke rose, hovered over the impact points for a moment, and then danced away with the wind in the rain.

If the impacts were close, they would check themselves for possible injuries. Often you didn't feel them because of the high adrenaline level. If you were unharmed, you would hastily look at the person next to you. This procedure had long since become second nature.

I sat in the trench with Ede and the rest of the men in our platoon who were fit to fight. We were waiting for the next wave of attacks. The chief instructor seemed more tense than usual. It was as if he felt responsible for everything and everyone since Zech's death. I left my seat and slid over to him. He clumsily pulled a cigarette out of his breast pocket, lit it, and held it in the palm of his hand with his thumb and forefinger so it wouldn't get wet. A cloud of blue haze rose and was immediately dispersed by the wind and rain.

"What do you think? Will they come?"

He looked at me questioningly. "You mean when will they come or who will attack this time? British, Indians or Canadians?"

I remained silent. We both knew my question was purely rhetorical. Ede finished his cigarette. He continued to raise his binoculars and survey the area. There was already a lot of rumbling over by 1st Company. He set the glass aside. "It won't be long now."

"Afraid for the boys?" I could see it in his eyes. His concern was undeniable.

"It's different when you're in charge. More and more of us old people are dying, and too many of the young. They are the ones who have to fill the gaps. It's cruel. The war robs them of many years. Either they grow old overnight or they die. Just like our motto in the Legion: "March or die!

How I had loved and hated that saying. On the march, we had grown together as a unit, and everyone stood up for everyone else. But those who were too weak in the end - we were buried in the desert.

Ede looked back over the edge of the trench. "Do you hear it?"

I listened. A heavy humming. Murmurs to our left and right. Frightened looks.

"Tanks?"

"I suppose so."

Wham ...

rrrt ... rrrrt

They were coming. The first tank shells hit well ahead of our positions, but they gave us an idea of the force with which they would hit us.

Infantry charged forward under the cover of heavy machine gun fire.

"Get ready, men!"

Erwin lay behind the MG 42, taking aim at the enemy from safe cover.

"Wait!" Ede ordered.

There was a crash all around us. The first shots were fired.

I aimed at the enemy. Smoke grenades were detonated. Thick clouds quickly formed, their gray billowing over the terrain.

"Now!"

The order to fire came late. We were almost out of sight. I pulled the trigger. One of the attackers fell to the ground, hit.

Erwin's MG 42 rattled and fired its deadly rounds. Shell after shell was ejected. The belt went through smoothly. The moon face had been very careful not to get any new ammunition boxes. The last shipment had many broken casings.

His machine gun and that of Master Sergeant Semmler's platoon were positioned to fire on the enemy from two sides, forcing them to retreat at best.

The attack petered out under the fire of our machine guns. For reasons unknown to us, the enemy tanks had not advanced any further. The fire gradually subsided. At this point we suspected a feint attack.

While the first wave of attacks was being repulsed, there was already a great deal of excitement in the company command post. The tank destroyer company had been completely reassembled and deployed nearby, as our reconnaissance troops suspected that the heaviest thrust would be on the outer flank. The conditions there were much better for the use of heavy vehicles and the troop movements were also stronger. In addition, our neighboring units were under constant artillery fire. This was a sure sign of an attack concentration.

Early reports of tank movements were sent from the outposts to the company command post via radio. As ordered, these reports were relayed by the rear guard. The expected responses did not materialize.

Lieutenant Kohler became enraged and vehemently demanded reinforcements to fight the tanks. He shoved the radio operator aside and shouted into the air himself: "If we are to hold the front, we urgently need tank destroyers or at least armor-piercing weapons. We can't stop steel hulks with our carbines!" He angrily handed the radio back to the operator and asked if the signalman had returned yet.

The telephone lines were down after the shelling. The strippers had already left in small groups. They followed the lines to find the damaged points and repair them. Detectives rushed around. Some of them fought their way through the area on foot, others on bicycles, but most of them raced along the roads on their DKW NZ 350s *(german motorcycle)*. Depending on the weather, they arrived at the command posts covered in dust, covered in dirt, or soaking wet, and delivered the most important news. Time and again, however, the dispatchers fell victim to enemy grenades, were captured by enemy shock troops, were captured by advancing troops, or were killed in accidents en route.

Lieutenant Kohler had been waiting for his signalman's return for some time and feared the worst. If the enemy found a way through with their tanks, the front would inevitably break.

"He's coming," were the relieving words of Sergeant Major Klemm.

With the company suffering so many casualties, every able-bodied man had to do what he could. In addition to Klemm, Lieutenant Kohler had brought three other men from the platoon to the company CP. Instead of being stationed three to four kilometers behind the HKL as they usually were during the battle, they were on duty here.

The detector looked exhausted. He was panting and gasping for breath. His uniform was torn at the knees and one sleeve. The private had a few scratches on his face.

"I was caught in the middle of an Ari attack. The British, or whoever was opposite us, fired too far. It was good for the comrades in the trench, but I was the one who suffered," he explained his appearance. "I had to jump from funnel to funnel and ..."

"That's all right," Kohler waved him off. "What report do you have from battalion?"

"We're getting a group of sappers. That's all they can give us to fight the tanks!"

The officer shook his head in astonishment. He couldn't understand why they were fighting the imminent danger with such weak forces. "Then all we can do is hope and pray!"

I never found out if Lieutenant Kohler prayed or not. The

constant rain had completely softened the terrain and the ground. Fortunately for us, the tank attack had bogged down. The heavy British tanks had gotten stuck in the mud during the attack. Many of them were bogged down.

In the second wave of the attack, the British infantry tried to create some kind of protective shield around the tanks that were unable to break free on their own.

Machine guns rattled, grenade launchers popped, and smaller and larger waves of attack were repulsed.

Pioneers had arrived. Their mission was to destroy as many trapped steel tanks as possible. I had to provide cover for the squad assigned to us and was also ordered to shoot any tank commander who stuck his head out of the turret. A counterattack by the company was to draw the enemy fire away from us. Once we got close enough, it was to start. It was a suicide mission.

While I checked my rifle and inserted a new loading strip, the sappers were getting ready. There was a sergeant, a private and two senior engineers, whose gray square star on their epaulettes looked quite new. A total of three mines were being prepared. I heard the grinding sound of the detonators being inserted. Each of these T-mines weighed 9 kg, 5 kg of which was explosive. The fourth sapper had only one fuse with 1 kg of explosives. This would not be enough to destroy a tank, but it was possible to blow off the track or, with a bit of luck, damage the engine when placed on the ventilation slots. They were also capable of rendering the tank's pipes useless with their explosive power.

The sergeant had recently been awarded the Iron Cross. At least that's what I assumed, since the ribbon was still shimmering in his buttonhole. "Ready?" he asked his men.

Glances at their watches followed. They all nodded. The tension was palpable. I turned and signaled to Ede. My pulse was beating like crazy again. I could feel my knees getting weak and my legs shaking slightly. I was glad when the barrage began and the first smoke grenades were thrown. With the detonations, this time the artificial smoke screen spread to our side. We scurried out of the position.

We oriented ourselves as far as possible along the flank. The noise of the battle increased. Our nerves were at the breaking point. First we crawled out of the positions on our stomachs, then we took the plunge and ran on crouching.

A distant "Hurraaaaa" could be heard, slightly distorted by the noise of the guns. Howitzers thundered. The counterattack was underway. We rose and rushed forward. I don't think I've ever been as scared as I was at that moment. I was expecting a hit at any moment, I thought we must be on the verge of enemy contact, but except for a fallen soldier, several banshees lying around, and piles of fired ammunition, there was nothing to see of the enemy.

The walls of fog had cleared, the barrage had subsided, and our comrades had retreated. We lay in safe cover, panting and breathing heavily. After our counterattack, the Bri-tish infantry had dug in on the opposite flank from us.

We could see four tanks. The sergeant peered over the cover. "Shermans. The Yanks have supplied the British with some of these behemoths. A 75mm cannon, a Browning machine gun with 12.7mm and two with 7.62mm. Five crew, the commander has a 360 degree mirror. If he looks out the hatch, you shoot him down."

The engineer looked cold as ice and seemed to know everything about the tank. He pulled out his binoculars.

"They're stuck. They can't get out without heavy equipment. We have to hurry. They won't be without infantry protection for long."

I brought my rifle forward and exposed the optics. A glance through the scope followed. Then I adjusted the sights. A second look. "I'm ready. How do we proceed? Should we wait for someone to lift the lid?"

She shook her head. "That takes too long. We can easily reach two of Tommy's ovens. We'll crack them. We can't get to the other two."

I hadn't heard the term "Tommy Stove" in a while. In Africa, the Shermans were nicknamed this because the ammunition inside the tank tended to ignite easily, which meant that the engines could also catch fire. A deadly scenario for the crew.

"We have to go for it, you take the cover."

I was stunned. "You want me to what?"

The sergeant gave me a look that reminded me of the field battalion sniper. "Shoot anything that might be dangerous to us!"

"How are you going to get it?"

"From behind!"

Before I could ask more questions, they were gone. I aimed my rifle at the four Sher-man tanks, one after the other. I couldn't see the four sappers anywhere. The machine guns rattled again. The barrage started again and I knew that a second diversionary attack was about to take place. Two of the Shermans turned their turrets. Although I had expected it, I jumped when the hatch of one of the more distant tanks was blown open. The commander cautiously stuck his head out and looked around. His head and shoulders were finally visible. I had him in my sights and wondered if it would be better to shoot or not. Which would do more damage to the sappers? After the tank commander put on his binoculars and obviously looked around, I decided to shoot. I aimed for the head. My legs started to shake again. I suppressed my shaking and took shallow breaths. He turned to the side. I put him down for a moment and took two deep breaths before aiming again. Stay calm. If he sees the Pioneers, they're as good as dead.

The head was right in the crosshairs. Inhale and exhale half your oxygen again. Hold your breath, your forefinger had reached the pressure point. I pulled it through. The shot cracked. I felt the recoil at my shoulder. The tank commander's head jerked to the side, his body crumpled abruptly inside the Sherman. A direct hit. Instinctively, I rolled to the side and shifted my position a few meters. I didn't feel very good and told myself that I had saved the lives of the sappers with that shot.

The moment I docked again, there was a huge rumble.

Thud.

A thick, dark mushroom cloud rose. Small explosions followed. I immediately spun around. Two engineers had blown up a Sherman. I hurried to the next tank. I saw the sergeant. He was close to the Sherman and had to see the welds on the steel giant. I had to admit that I lacked the courage for such a task.

Meanwhile the destroyed tank was in flames. I didn't see any of the crew get out. The Sherman had become the grave of the five men.

The tank crew of the intact Sherman responded with random fire. Muzzle flashes flashed from the barrels of their guns. The rearmost tank had started its engine and tried to break free of the mud, but only sank deeper.

The commander of the Sherman, urged on by the sergeant and the man next to him, pushed back the hatch. He tried to explore the area with a scissor scoop. At that moment, the sergeant jumped up, followed shortly by his companion. The British tank commander recognized the danger, jumped up and raised a machine pistol. My shot hit him at the same moment. I shot him in the jaw. The submachine gun fell to the ground. The tanker stood paralyzed in the hatch. I repeated for a second shot. The sappers were close enough to the tank. Both detonated their explosives. The T-mine was balanced on the back and slid towards the turret. The detonator landed on the rear track.

Both lancers turned and ran away. The rearmost, stuck Sherman had turned its turret. Small flames danced at the muzzle as the grenade left the barrel. They seemed to merge seamlessly into gunpowder vapor.

The two explosions of the explosives merged with the impact of the tank shell.

Wham - wham - wham.

The tank rose and fell. It was now leaning slightly. The turret was no longer properly seated on the chassis. A man disembarked.

The tank shell had missed its target by far. Two smoke grenades were thrown. They detonated between 4 and 7 seconds after being thrown. The burning of the mixture of he-xachloroethane and zinc powder would again create a saving smoke screen for two minutes.

I lost sight of the pioneers in the fog. When it lifted, all hell broke loose. British infantrymen ran toward the tanks. Two light machine guns moved into position.

Rumble

The shells of the burning Sherman had exploded. The wreckage had become a blazing fireball.

I took aim at one of the machine gunners. The distance was very long, but I took a chance and fired a shot.

I missed. I had recklessly fired that shot as my second from the same position.

Bang!

The tank shell exploded only 20 meters from me. Shrapnel scratched my steel helmet. Goose bumps covered my entire body. I made myself small and crawled back into the mud, looking for better cover.

Three of the four pioneers returned. One looked extremely battered and pale as a sheet. His face was covered with scratches and a deep cut. He sat down. Their bodies were struggling for oxygen.

"Where's Lehmann?" gasped the sergeant.

The one with the furrowed face answered. Blood rushed into his mouth. He spat out the red juice and ran his hands over his face. A dirty, bloody stain remained.

"Don't, you'll get blood poisoning," the priest scolded.

"Lehmann was too slow. He got stuck in the mud and couldn't throw himself down in time," the injured man gushed. His voice cracked. "The damn mine blew up in our faces. I managed to place mine well, but Lehmann's..." he sobbed.

"It's all right, Otto," the corporal comforted him, soaking his handkerchief with water from the canteen and wiping his wounds.

"Ouch!"

"I added a little schnapps to the water. That disinfects it."

"Go on!" the sergeant urged, looking at me and nodding. That probably meant something like: well done.

I had images of the tank commander with his jaw shot off. I turned away and threw up.

I had seen worse, but I had done that to that man. Cursed war.

Wham - wham - wham

There were several explosions between us and the British infantry. Machine guns rattled.

"These are ours. Come on, we have to go back!"

The private passed the handkerchief to the chief engineer. "Hold it there. There's a lot of blood, but it's only a small wound."

The sergeant kept a constant eye on the surroundings through his binoculars. The noise of the battle grew louder and louder. "They're coming!" he said.

I grabbed my rifle and immediately remembered the sniper instructor's warning.

Get rid of your rifle and anything that identifies you as a sniper ... the rifle will be rammed up your ass ... tortured to death ....

The thought scared me.

And if they beat my guts out of my body, I won't throw a-way my rifle, I decided, thinking of my comrades, the dirt they were lying in, and the shrapnel from the British shells that tore us apart. Anger rose in me. Unbridled rage.

"I'll take as many as I can..."

The sergeant cut me off. "Not the Tommys, our men."

Hope and fighting spirit had returned with the burning tanks. The dark columns of smoke led the way, and the companies in our section had launched a massive counterattack. The British withdrew. We had held the front line and had not allowed a breach.

The next few days passed with light or medium artillery fire. The front was never quiet. The defensive successes brought a brief euphoria, but this faded noticeably with the cold and the constant rain.

It was worst at night. Hunger plagued us, and despite the temporary shelters we had built and sealed with canvas, the water found its way everywhere and found us. The first absences were due to illness. And everyone was waiting for us to be taken out and moved to the back.

"At least we'll be spared any more scouting parties for the time being," Krueger muttered, rubbing his stomach. "I'm so hungry. It's about time the food carriers arrived."

We crouched under a wooden shed, the sides of which we had sealed as well as we could with canvas to protect us from the wind and rain. A few loose planks lay on the completely soaked and muddy ground. They were supposed to keep us from sinking into the soft ground. When you walked on them, they sank and a dirty film of water covered them. Sitting in this position was anything but pleasant. But it was far better than the foxholes and shelters in the barren rock of Monte Natale.

The Allies had fired their howitzers not only at the positions, but also at our supply routes. As a result, ammunition and supplies could only be transported after dark.

Krueger had to wait another hour before we finally heard the relieving clattering and groaning that mixed with the splashing as the food transporters' boots landed in the muddy water.

"Black train?" grunted a deep voice from the darkness.

"You've come to the right place," Krueger replied. "Keep the munchies coming."

Six men marched up in a row. Their outlines were barely visible in the faint moonlight.

"It's about time. We're starving already," the lance corporal added.

The first food carrier had stopped. "It's no fun dragging all this crap through the pitch-black night. I've already been hit on the head twice," the soldier with the deep bass voice grumbled back.

"Thresher? Is that you?" asked Krueger. The tone of his voice had changed. It was more polite than before.

"Krueger, you old bastard. You're indestructible too."

They both laughed and shook hands.

"Help me get my pack off."

Krueger stood behind the food carrier and grabbed the container, while the grumpy Landser undid the buckle of the wide hip belt and slipped out of the straps. The lance corporal set the container down.

"Ah, that's good."

The other food carriers were quickly surrounded and distributed.

"Golly, Drescher, I thought you'd been hit hard. According to the latrine slogans, you came to the hospital with a Heimatschuss."

"Heimatschuss, ha ha," came the reply with a deep, resounding laugh. "I was in Bavaria for six weeks, then went to the Black Forest for four weeks to recuperate, and after fourteen days' leave they took me back. I can no longer walk like a horse, but I can pull like a donkey." Deep laughter rang through the stables again. "Imagine, they wanted to train me to be a doctor. I declined with thanks."

"What's for lunch?"

"Pea stew with sausage, but it's so watery you don't need anything else to drink, and you're still not thirsty. The food hasn't improved."

"Never mind, I'm hungry as a wolf."

"But the commissary bread is fresh and we have some red wine with us. Every other water bottle is filled with it."

The food carrier was called. "Drescher, we must go on, the others want to eat too!"

Krueger held out his hand. "Take care of yourself, you're a good guy."

"Likewise."

Shake hands.

Ede and I were already ready with the cooking utensils. "Krueger, unscrew the aluminum container, we're hungry too."

"I'll have a sip of wine first," the mute grumbled, which meant that he had talked a lot for him.

March 5th, 1944

Since yesterday, the division has been taken out one by one. Today it was our turn and we were happy to finally be taken out of the front line. We didn't know if it was a tribute from the British or if they had simply run out of ammunition. But as we cleared the positions, the guns fell silent.

A few miles behind the front line we were billeted for the next 14 days. It wasn't very fancy, but it was dry and warm. I felt like I was in Pa-radise.

After the barracks-like commissary had also returned, we stood in line for the barber, dentist, and field doctor. With a proper haircut and our wounds treated, we finally got two days off, but we weren't allowed to stray too far from the troops.

There was field mail and I was able to write my mother a long and above all legible letter again. I left many notes unnoticed, glossing over the life of a compatriot at the front to take away some of her grief and worry.

It was with great sadness that I read that my brother Oskar had succumbed to his wounds. As I looked around at my comrades who were all reading their letters for the second or third time, I recognized joy and sorrow. The postal service was our link to home. While some, like me, experienced sadness, others re-joiced. One of my comrades became a father, another got the "yes" from his fiancée to get married.

Only a few comrades were out and about during their free time. Two young guys had made several attempts to meet nurses from the field hospital. They returned with disappointed faces. The girls either didn't have time or the boys were too young for them.

"Be happy," they were comforted by Krueger. "Remember the ointment, it burns like hell on your penis."

After two days of rest, the next tour of duty began with a great deal of equipment fuss. The whistles were blown inces-santly, resulting in an extra field exercise. The post-duty flap-ping took place after the lunch break, so the slobs among us had to wolf down their food to have time for equipment maintenance.

The food wasn't much better, but since it was only a short walk to the field kitchen, it was hot.

In the evenings we sat together and played cards or talked.

March 17th, 1944

The low pressure system had finally moved out. With the beautiful weather of the high pressure area, our order to leave also arrived. Completely exhausted and decimated, Regiment 361 was finally withdrawn from the theater and moved to the Nettuno/Rome area on the west coast of Italy.

Because of the constant air-raid alert, we left at dusk. The drivers were ordered to use only camouflage lights. They drove with appropriate caution. It also proved to be an advantage that they kept a sufficient distance to the vehicle in front. Some of the roads were extremely full of craters, often only provisionally filled with stones or earth. If the vehicle in front braked, it was difficult to see because of the camouflage lighting.

The drivers gave it their all and took us across the boot from the Adriatic to the Mediterranean. We only stopped to refuel or when we had to stop for a troop transport to the HKL. Field policemen kept order at crossroads and busy places.

We used the breaks to stretch our legs or relieve ourselves. By the time we reached our destination the next morning, the drivers were exhausted and we had calluses on our buttocks. The nearly 300 kilometers across the Italian boot had exhausted everyone. To everyone's amazement, we had no breakdowns. There were no breakdowns, air raids or other incidents that would have forced us to make an emergency stop.

We were stationed near Nettuno as a reserve unit. The HKL of the Gustav Line was about 100 km away, but the landing area of the Americans at Anzio was only a few kilometers away. They had been bogged down there since January. They had not succeeded in extending the beachhead to completely cut off German supplies from the Cassino front, let alone encircle the German troops. The latter would have been an attempt to create a second Stalingrad.

However, the OKW had also failed to push the American troops back into the sea. A kind of stalemate had developed. And so, despite the Allied bridgehead, all was quiet. Even the dreaded fighter-bombers flew over us instead of attacking us.

The quartermaster had done a good job. We were billeted in a large house. The Italian family hadn't moved out. They didn't want to leave their property, which I could understand. There were a few olive trees in the garden, two cypresses and several citrus trees next to vegetable plots. In short, a Mediterranean landscape. Hot summers and heavy winter rains provided the best conditions for a good harvest.

Although Alfredo Russo was officially the head of the family, it was his wife who ruled here. When she spoke, everyone was on their toes. Alfredo was a slender man, his wife an real Italian m

Mama: Pitch-black hair, pinned up, overweight, but still very agile and extremely likeable.

When we introduced ourselves as forced boarders, she smiled, shrugged, and we were met with a torrent of words. Alfredo spoke a little German and said curtly: "You should call her Mama or Mama Russo. And you are very welcome."

"Was that all?" asked Krueger. "She talked for what seemed like five minutes."

Alfredo fidgeted a little, looked at his wife, received a firm nod, and looked back at Krueger. "If you want to join us for dinner, you have to get the food. We eat on time. Il pranzo, lunch, is served at 14:00. Dinner, la cena, is served on time at 7:30. If you're not there, you get nothing."

Mama Russo put her hands on her hips and looked at her guests.

Krueger scratched his head. "Sounds like my house."

We laughed.

"And you have to keep it clean. She gets mad if the house is dirty."

"That's clear," said Erwin Muller, his face glowing red.

Six men found a wonderful place to live here for the next few months. I was one of them.

Everyday military life had us firmly in its grip. With the first enlistment, supplies were brought in again. This time it consisted of young recruits as well as those returning from the military hospitals. Slightly wounded soldiers who remained with the troops were assigned to the company's troop units.

These were the combat troop with the field kitchen, the two rations troops I and II, and the baggage troop, which also included the workers whose main task was to keep the company mobile by repairing the vehicles. The troop was led by Sergeant Major Klemm.

The command of the troop changed from company to battalion or regiment, depending on whether it was a war of movement, a war of position, or a rest period. Our lieutenant, and therefore the company sergeant, was currently in command.

Lieutenant Kohler still commanded the company as acting commander. His second-in-command was a slightly wounded officer's cadet with the rank of corporal. He limped slightly with his left foot.

We received word from Captain Geller that he had come through an operation well and would probably be out of action for another four to six weeks.

Instead of four, our company was reduced to three infantry platoons for manpower reasons. Our platoon was also reduced to two groups. My old group consisted of the two Lance Corporals Krueger and the moon-faced Erwin Mueller, as well as the taciturn Private Buchecker. Then there was Elmar Roeder and Kraus, the only uninjured young Landser from the last reinforcement, who had recently joined us. New to us were the young soldiers Ferber and Merk, as well as Privat First Class Schmitz, who had returned to the front after being wounded for some time. As a sniper, I was no longer officially part of the group, but was still assigned to the company. I was all the happier to be able to stay with my comrades in the Russo family.

Corporal Krueger acted as group leader, Erwin was his deputy.

The three new members of the group, together with two men from the second group, were housed in one of the neighboring houses.

"Fall in!"

The Spitfire's voice made us jump every time. As usual, he walked down the rows, greeting the newcomers with the same words he had used to welcome us a few weeks before.

Welcome to life, welcome to the barracks, welcome to drill. I was glad to be able to avoid most of the field exercises by saying goodbye to Ede and his bles-sing, and to the company commander with his camouflage and shooting exercises.

When the men came out of the compound in the evening, completely exhausted and in dirty uniforms, Mama Russo was waiting for us. With a look worse than our spit, she made sure we didn't carry any dirt in our boots into the house.

Krueger lived up to his organizational skills. While we were still being fed from the field kitchen at noon, he had managed to get something for Mama Russo to cook almost every day. Accordingly, the food was steaming from huge pots and smelled like a gourmet restaurant.

Alfredo was not stingy with his wine and grappa supplies, and we contributed all kinds of market produce. So every evening was like a little party with our host family.

We learned that Mama Russo and Alfredo had three children. Their son had been an officer in Mussolini's army and had died in Africa. His picture with a black bar was on the mantel in the large living room. Her two daughters were married. One lived on a farm about 40 kilometers from here, the other in Rome. There were three grandchildren.

Mama Russo missed her children and probably saw the young recruit Kraus or Elmar Roeder as her son. In any case, both received special attention.

Although the American landing zone was less than six kilometers from here, the war was far away for us during those 14 days. The Mediterranean climate, the noticeably stronger sun and the warmth of Mama Russo made us forget the daily grind of war.

In addition to training recruits, the division also had the task of protecting the coast. This duty was comparable to guard duty in the barracks. Our company was called up only once for a 48-hour cover. Otherwise we were spared from guard duty.

March 31st, 1944

Reality caught up with us sooner than we would have liked. Although the training level of the newly formed 90th Panzergrenadier Division was more than poor, we were transferred inland. In the mountains between Rome and Ortona there had been an increase in gang attacks on our supply lines. The partisans struck at night, blowing up tracks or supply depots and attacking smaller columns in company strength.

Partisans were feared and hated. They could be behind any facade, including those of Alfredo and Mama Russo. But I ruled them both out. You couldn't go crazy. In gang warfare, war showed its darkest side. Our opponent wore no uniform and was not in any position. Partisans lived at home or in large hidden camps. A farmer's son could be a partisan, as well as his mother or grandfather. During the day they smiled at you, at night they slit your throat. The enemy had no face.

I found retaliation equally despicable. I hoped never to find myself in such a situation. Hoping to be exempted, I tried to get a proper sniper course. To that end, I went to the office to ask the spit for an opportunity. As I was standing in front of the door, I heard a phone call. Klemm was calling a pioneer unit where some of our men were training. The comrades had to stop the training immediately and return to the troops. Disappointed, I abandoned my plans and turned around. Tonight there would be another excellent meal and plenty of red wine at Mama Russo's.

The unpleasant task of fighting the gangs passed the battalion's snipers by. While our comrades were moving through difficult terrain, searching for partisans in mountain villages and locating their hiding places, we had to report to our respective company squads.

We were assigned to protect the routes to the battalion and regimental headquarters, to accompany the field post transports as snipers, and to protect ammunition and supplies of all kinds.

On the first few trips, I was still extremely nervous. I wondered what the difference was between a normal Landser sitting in the cab for protection and a sniper.

The drivers reassured me. "Don't worry, buddy, the gangs only attack at night. We're safe."

They were right. I made some nice comrades and was glad not to be fighting gangs.

After ten days, a rumor started circulating. While our company had still not found any guerrillas, a neighboring company was said to have found something. A rifle had been found in a farmhouse during a search. The old farmer assured them that it was a hunting rifle, but the officer leading the squad did not believe him. The old Italian's daughter came along and began cursing at the German soldiers. The officer then had them both tied up and ordered them shot. He considered it proven that the small mountain farm was a partisan nest.

Ten soldiers were assigned to the firing squad. Two of them shot the farmer, while the other eight soldiers deliberately missed.

After a moment of shock, the young woman insulted the soldiers. The officer was furious and shot the alleged partisan with a submachine gun. He then threatened to court-martial the men for disobeying orders, but he could not prove who had disobeyed the order by shooting past.

We wanted to get to the bottom of it and find out more, but we couldn't find out which platoon it was. Even Krueger, who came back with all kinds of new information about his raids on the supply depots, kept shaking his head. "Nobody knows anything. Maybe it's not true."

The fact was, we were relieved shortly after the rumor started. We never found out if it had anything to do with the incident. A few days later, another part of the story was added. It was said that the officer had been mysteriously killed in a skirmish with partisans. Allegedly, he had received a few blows to the back. This latrine slogan was also never officially confirmed.

April 11th, 1944

The situation on the Cassino front became increasingly tense. The enemy pressed relentlessly, overwhelmingly and with concentrated force against our positions. The OKW also expected a second landing attempt by the Allies. In this case, or in case of an optional airborne landing by the enemy, we were to carry out the counterattack. The 90th Panzergrenadier Division was also the reserve for the Gustav Line. On paper, we were an almost elite division that had proven itself in battle.

The fact that we had suffered enormous losses in recent weeks and had reached the limits of our capacity was swept under the carpet by the authorities.

Germany was bled dry. The gaping personnel holes were still being filled with very young recruits. They had just completed their labor service and then received three to six months of basic training before being sent to the front. They were anything but trained soldiers, and we had to teach them everything they needed to know to survive in a very short time.

It was impossible to think of full-fledged men for a combat mission, let alone give the recruits a chance of survival in close combat. Yesterday they were holding pencils and rulers, tomorrow they would be ramming a bayonet into the stomach of a Tommy or an American.

These young men were victims of the Hitler regime. Ideologically imbued with Nazi ideas from an early age, they were sent to the front to die. It was up to us to delay that as long as possible. That too is a merciless face of war.

With new marching orders, we were housed in old manor houses about 12 km south of Rome. They were empty and supposedly belonged to the Italian King Victor Emmanuel III.

Our mission had not changed. We were still the intervention

reserve for the front and were to destroy possible landing attempts by sea and air.

Major General Baade continued to insist on constant training of the troops. Everyone was trained without exception, not just the recruits. I couldn't get out of it either and had to go to the night exercises.

Because of the night exercises, we inevitably had a little more free time during the day. Krueger used this time for his organizational activities. On the third day he returned with a cow and a pig. The sow was on the back of an old SPA truck. The engine still had to be started with a hand crank and rattled louder than two machine guns firing continuously. The truck moved so slowly that the cow dutifully trotted along behind it. Krueger grinned broadly and pressed something into the driver's hand. I couldn't see what it was, but I assumed it was cash. After a scrutinizing look, the money went into the driver's pocket. Then the two of them talked for a while. Krueger took a piece of paper, reached into his pocket again and gave the driver more money. Then they shook hands and the corporal got out.

In the meantime, five or six Landser had gathered at the SPA. Some were examining the animals, others were admiring the old truck.

"Get to work, boys. Get the pig down, but don't let her run away! My new Italian friend has to stay behind the wheel and keep accelerating. If the truck goes down, it's no fun getting it up again. The thing kicks back". Krueger pointed to the opening for the hand crank on the front of the SPA *(italian truck)*.

Erwin Mueller's face glowed fiery red as usual. The Upper Bavarian rubbed his hands together in anticipation. "Kettle soup tomorrow!"

We slaughtered on our day off. We found everything we needed in the kitchens and outbuildings of the houses. We used an old wood-fired wash kettle as a soup kettle. Everyone helped with the butchering, and the inimitable smell of freshly made kettle soup spread good cheer everywhere. In addition to the field exercises, such activities helped the group to grow together.

Later, as we enjoyed the last of the market goods we had been given, Krueger told us about a wine cellar. "The cellar is full of wine. We don't even have to go far."

"You know what looting means?" Ede asked.

Krueger waved him off. "Plunder," he said with the expression of a clown. "Who said anything about looting? We go there, invite people and ..."

"That's looting!"

The lance corporal raised his hands protectively in front of him, as if to ward off an attack. "Let me finish," he defended himself. "We're leaving barter goods."

Surprised faces.

"Barter goods?" asked Ede.

Krueger had his typical grin on his face again. The look was mischievous. "All I need is two or three men to accompany me and a truck, or even better, two trucks."

Ede had doubts. "The risk is too high."

I gave myself a jolt. "I'll go with you. I'm sure I have something in my backpack to trade."

"Sounds like a legionnaire's mission," Erwin laughed. "I can't miss it."

"Jo," the mute nodded.

Ede shook his head. "You're crazy!"

"Legionnaire's mission," the moon face repeated.

"I would come too," said Elmar Roeder.

Ede put his foot down. "You have too much to lose. You stay here. If someone asks for us, you'll think of something." He turned to us. "Legionnaire's mission," he mimicked Erwin, trying to imitate a Bavarian accent and failing with much laughter. "You're a bunch of fools. Of course I'm with you. I have to keep an eye on you."

The Legion - one for all - all for one. Our motto is still alive.

"But I wasn't in the Legion," Krueger tried to say, but he

was overheard as the men raised their glasses in celebration.

"To Krueger!"

The old warhorse had actually managed to get two trucks. They arrived at nightfall on the very first night without night training.

"I know the drivers well. They can shut up and get a share."

Krueger acted like a businessman who had contacts everywhere and kept them going with small and large donations.

"Are they reliable? I have no desire to answer to a court martial."

"Don't worry about it. I know both drivers very well. I went to school with one of them, and the other is related to me by three corners. I'm sure they'll keep their mouths shut."

That was enough to calm Ede. The Opel Blitz stopped. Both drivers got out, greeted Krueger with a friendly handshake, and then greeted us.

One of the drivers even looked a little like Krueger. I guessed it was his distant cousin. He spoke up. "I've been looking at the route. We can use some back roads. The chain dogs are only at the major intersections."

We hadn't thought about night patrols by the field police. I thought for a moment about what excuse we could use, but that was no longer valid when the driver continued to talk.

"I have my connections there, and one of the field gendarmes owes me a favor. I'll give him a bottle of wine and we'll call it even."

Now I realized that this man must be Krueger's relative. Organizing, bribing, and making deals must be in the blood of this family.

We split into the two trucks and drove off. Despite being well prepared and halfway bribed by the field gendarmes, I felt a little uneasy about the whole thing.

The side roads marked on the map were nothing more than impassable, wide dirt tracks designed for donkey carts. The two

Opel Blitz cars bounced up and down accordingly. As soon as the men behind the steering wheels rounded one pothole, they plunged into the next. After a few miles I was more afraid of burst tires than of field policemen or partisans.

When we stopped and Krueger shouted that we had reached our destination, I was relieved. We were in a wine-growing area. Krueger walked a few meters to the left, then turned around and walked down a small path between two fields of vines. Shortly after that, a whistle sounded. "Over here. I've found the entrance."

We found a really rich harvest. The owner had built a real wine and ham bunker out here and had probably hidden a lot of his possessions. One thing was clear to me: Anyone who had that much was not poor. So I didn't feel bad about this little raid.

It was well after midnight when we began our journey home. We were laughing, in high spirits, and looking forward to eating our fat haul. We had loaded more than 2000 liters of wine and about 8 kilograms of the best bacon.

On the way back, the two drivers were very careful to avoid potholes. This time it would have been fatal to hit something and cause a break.

We arrived undisturbed at the manor houses around three in the morning. The drivers got their share, plus a bonus for the informant of the chain dogs. The rest was divided among us.

"I hope we stay here for a while," Ede grinned and uncorked a bottle of wine after everything was stowed away. "Cheers, men!"

May 10th, 1944

As the wind blew from the south, we could hear the thunder of the guns. We suspected that the warm, dry weather would force the enemy to break through; we had been holding him back at the Gustav Line for half a year. He was far superior to us in everything. The Allies were constantly adding troops, seemed to have an endless supply of artillery and ammunition, and clearly had air superiority. Their fighter-bombers could fly freely over Italy, bombing our front positions and supply lines. If you saw one of our fighters in the sky, you could see a tenfold superiority of the enemy approaching shortly afterwards.

The time for rest was over. When the Spiess ordered the company to line up and Lieutenant Kohler announced the new marching orders, we knew that the decisive battle for Cassino and the entire Gustav Line had begun.

We immediately moved to Frosinone in the Liri Valley, about 80 kilometers away. The trip took two days. The reason was once again the air superiority of the Allies. Their fighters and fighter-bombers kept circling to destroy the supply columns. After a few unavoidable air raids, we drove only at night, and this time we had no breakdowns.

When we reached the area of operations, we heard the incessant thundering and crashing. Lightning flashed on the horizon. All hell had broken loose at the front. By now it was clear to all of us that the carefree time of goulash and wine in the king's mansions was finally over. Just one day later, it continued.

The 44th Infantry Division Hoch- und Deutschmeister held the front around the village of Pignataro and was completely exsanguinated. The unit had to be removed from the front immediately. We relieved them and filled the gap to repel the massive Allied attacks together with the 15th Panzer Division and the 1st Parachute Infantry Division. The faces of their comrades were relieved, but also petrified and still full of fear. Their eyes reflected what they had experienced, they were expressionless. When we slammed the doors of the trucks too hard, some of them flinched. They came from the hell we had just walked into.

We were caught in the middle of the enemy's decisive offensive. At 23:00 hours on May 11, a massive artillery bombardment began. Ship's guns and artillery bombarded a section of the front more than 30 kilometers wide. The earth shook from Minturno on the coast to Monte Cassino. The 8th British Army and the 5th US Army trained the barrels of over 1,600 guns on the German positions, preparing a massive infantry attack with this thunderclap.

We were in the Liri Valley, right in the middle of the cannon fire. The regiment was right at the interface between the British and the Americans. Our battalion positions were being attacked by units of the 78th British Infantry Division.

It couldn't have been worse. We were no strangers to artillery fire, but nothing compared to this inferno. The pitch-black sky flashed and twitched incessantly. It was like a thunderstorm, except instead of rain, it was explosives, shrapnel, and pressure waves. In short, death. The howling of the approaching shells and the thousands of detonations combined to create an indescribable hellish noise that paralyzed every fiber in our bodies, made our muscles tremble uncontrollably, and put a bell of fear over us from which we could not free ourselves.

Apart from the detonations of the large-caliber shells or the mass explosions of the smaller ones, the phosphorus shells were the ones we feared the most. They caused fires and even minimal skin contact resulted in wounds that were difficult to heal. If you tried to hit a burning spot on your body with your hand, the burning mass would stick to it and the fire would spread further. The hand burned mercilessly, sometimes to the bone. It was a cruel death sentence on the battlefield. I saw burning men jump up. They hoped for a saving shot. If it wasn't the fire that killed them, it was the fumes from the phosphorus shells. They were poisonous. If you inhaled them, the agony lasted several days before you died horribly.

Our fear was all the greater when we saw the fires caused by these grenades blazing. Grown men began to weep. Many wet themselves, and even convinced unbelievers began to pray. It is almost impossible to describe the hell we were in.

As the artillery fire moved further back, we realized that the infantry was advancing. And when it died down completely, we knew they were here. Now it was time to bring out the learned automatism of the soldier. Scanning to see if you were injured and hadn't noticed because of your adrenaline level was the beginning. This was followed by a check of weapons and equipment. How were the neighbors? Did they need help or were they ready for action?

"Attention!" was announced. "They're coming!"

We didn't have time to digest the fear of the artillery strike. It had to be suppressed and made room for the fear of the impending attack.

"Group Krueger to me!" I heard from the left.

"Assemble 2nd Company!"

I was unhurt. Calls for medics came from all directions. I wanted to jump up and run away, but I couldn't. I had to fight, had to stand up to the onrushing priority. Doubts overcame me. Doubt and pure fear. My whole body was shaking and I could not move.

I don't know if it was a few seconds, minutes or half an hour. There was a small thud next to me. I was startled. Ede had jumped into my cover hole and hit me in the shoulder.

"You okay?"

I looked at the headmaster, swallowed the lump in my throat and nodded. "Y ... Yes," I croaked with a dry throat.

Ede pointed to my canteen. "Have a drink, then we need you!"

British pioneers crawled forward on their bellies. With the help of wire cutters, they overcame the first barbed-wire entanglements, then planted explosives in the dense, sharp-edged barrier. The explosions mingled with the artillery fire, but they did not go unnoticed.

Again and again we raised our heads to see the blown passages in the shimmering, flashing light. Dark figures followed the pioneers in company. The soldiers squeezed through the narrow corridors. In a few minutes the magic would begin. Just beyond the wire entanglement was a minefield. As soon as they reached it and the first mines detonated, flares would shoot up and bathe the land ahead in a bizarrely bright light. Machine guns would rattle and their rounds would roll down the enemy.

My job was to find and eliminate the subleaders, platoon leaders, and company commanders.

I dared to look at the enemy again and raised my head above cover as a large-caliber grenade landed nearby.

Boom!

Stones and dirt came crashing down on me, and the ground shook for a moment. I instinctively ducked. The acrid smell of gunpowder smoke made it hard to breathe. The loud bang had barely died down when the screams of the wounded began. Behind me, a commotion began. Men were running around. Medics scurried through the craters looking for the poor guys who had been hit. One of them wouldn't stop screaming. Long, drawn-out screams alternated with cries for his mother. Eventually, the screaming degenerated into whimpering and moaning until it stopped altogether.

"Either he's dead or the paramedics gave him morphine," I thought, feeling a slight tremor in my knees. I was scared. Scared to death.

This last powerful impact ended the artillery fire.

Wham ... wham ...

Mines detonated.

They're here, it flashed through me!

"Look out!" shouted Ede.

I was glad to hear his voice. He was closer to where the big suitcase hit than I was, and he seemed to have remained unharmed.

Exampel Photo – german warning signs
panel-1451328_1920
Pixabay Lizenz: *https://pixabay.com/de/service/license/*

"Fire only on command!"

Gun barrels were pushed over trench edges and cover holes. Crews of antitank guns got ready. Machine guns moved into position and grenade launchers prepared to fire.

"Wait!"

It was nerve-wracking.

Boom!

The wind carried the cries of the Tommys to us. They were the same poor bastards we were. I remember how we sang Christmas carols together in Africa during a truce, only to bang our heads again three days later. The Cassino front is an insatiable juggernaut that feeds on people. And today was battle day.

"Nooooow!"

The call was loud and prolonged. At the same time, a flare gun was raised. The cartridge fizzed into the night, ignited, and cast a wavering, bright screen of light over the land. We recognized the approaching British soldiers in the artificial magnesium light. They were advancing across the plain. The area was cordoned off and we were in the hills to the left and right.

Shots rang out. Machine guns began to fire, spinning deadly webs with their tracer bullets. Bodies fell to the ground. Men threw themselves to the ground and took cover. Mines detonated. The British ran into a wall of steel.

The light went out. Immediately, three or four more flares shot up in quick succession. The enemy had caught up. A second company moved up. Muzzle flashes.

I was lying with my rifle ready, looking through the scope. One of the British made hand signals, waving men over to him. I could only see the soldier's hand and shoulder as he aimed at the broad shoulder and pulled the trigger. The hand dropped with a jerk. Hit! The lights went out again. The noise of the battle grew.

Ede came running up and threw himself beside me. "We got them," he rasped. I pointed at my ears to let him know I couldn't hear him. The noise was too much. "We - are you able to locate the radio operator or an officer?" Ede shouted now to drown out the noise.

"No, not really!"

He patted me on the shoulder. "Keep looking!"

Ede scampered off again and I started shooting. I shot indiscriminately at all the men I had in my sights. I took aim, saw movement or a muzzle flash, took aim and pulled the trigger. I fired three magazines and then slid down. As I slid the fourth clip in, the fire died down a bit. The attack had stalled.

Only our machine guns were still hammering their rounds out of the barrels.

With the next flare we could see that the enemy was retreating.

"Hurraaaa!" came from the positions.

I took a deep breath, but suspected that this could only be a prelude to the attack. A heavy artillery barrage like this was guaranteed to lead to something bigger.

Medics rushed through the ranks again. Somewhere in the darkness I saw cigarettes glowing. The men's faces glowed orange as they puffed.

The muffled sound of engines and a metallic clattering grew

louder. Tanks were rolling toward us.

During the battle, those damn sappers had cleared the barbed wire enough to create one or two armored passages. Sherman M4 A 4s with mounted mine flails led the way, followed by main battle tanks and infantry close behind.

"Clearance tank!"

"Tank attack!"

The call went out for tank destroyers, but they were not here. The first Paks fired.

Thud.

The tank destroyers reached the minefield. Like wild furies, their iron mine flails plowed through the earth, detonating one mine after another. Small pieces of shrapnel scraped against the steel armour.

The Shermans stopped and took aim at the Pak's muzzle flashes.

Bang!

Infantry followed, this time trying to advance through the high ground.

Explosion after explosion resounded. Tank shells, exploding mines, and Pak bullets exploded in rows. A tank had caught fire. Flames flickered from the wreckage and lit up the area around the blazing steel giant. Our machine gun positions resumed their fire, once again weaving the deadly web over the Liri Valley, clearly visible through the tracer ammunition. Again and again they tore holes in the infantry squads seeking cover behind the advancing tanks.

The men in the grenade launchers fired grenade after grenade from the barrels.

Wham ... wham ... wham!

One of the grenades had detonated next to a moving tank, breaking its track. Within the next minute, the colossus was stuck. Chain links whizzed around like deadly bullets.

On the flank, the British threatened to break through and were pushed back by a hastily formed reserve unit, including a tank group from our neighboring division.

By morning we had reached the end of our strength. Some of our men slept from exhaustion as they lay in position. Burnt out tank wrecks were smoldering. There was an acrid smell in the air. The ground around us was riddled with craters. Fallen soldiers lay scattered across the battlefield. Some of their limbs were stiffly stretched upward, as if reaching for the sky. Now and then someone stirred. The wounded who had not been found during the night whimpered and moaned.

In an act of mercy, a brief truce was agreed to allow the poor devils to recover.

"Sleep in two rhythms" was announced.

Those who could still stand on their feet were told to stay in position, those who had reached the end of their strength were to sleep. We were separated into two groups.

"Change in three hours!"

From a human point of view, it was almost impossible to hold the front for any length of time without replacements, but we had no other choice. With seven casualties, our company's losses were still below average. Fortunately, there were no casualties reported from my old group.

The truce was immediately put to good use by our food carriers. The comrades in the field kitchens and the butcher and bakery shops had to work through the night. This time the coffee and stew were hot, the bread still warm from baking. Dirty fingers reached for cooking utensils. We devoured the food greedily. After all, it might be our last.

There was another little surprise. Klemm and Lieutenant Kohler had come to Ede to congratulate him. He had been awarded the Iron Cross First Class. "We'll celebrate that here after this battle," laughed Klemm and patted our schoolmaster on the shoulder. The ceremony lasted less than five minutes, then they both moved on. They awarded four more Iron Crosses.

I couldn't tell if Ede was proud of the award or didn't care. He sat down almost without reacting and ate his stew.

After the meal, I was very tired and regretted having signed up for the group that was supposed to stay awake at the beginning. I lay in my position and refused to close my eyes. I kept getting up and jumping around for a few minutes. I crossed my arms in front of my chest as if doing gymnastics and then pulled them apart again. Some of the soldiers smiled, others imitated me. I pushed sleep aside for a few minutes and watched the area in front of me. It was depressing to watch the recovery of the severely wounded and fallen. I wondered how many of these men I had killed. My thoughts circled.

If every shot I fired was a hit, then .... No, not every shot was a hit. There were certainly misses. How many loading strips had I used?

I looked at the many dead bodies. Surely some had been recovered during the battle. So there must have been more.

How many Britons had Erwin shot with his machine gun?

With this thought, the numbers I attributed to myself began to dwindle.

How many mothers had to weep now? What suffering did this region bring to the world? Why did we have to lie here in the dirt and give our lives for something we didn't want? I myself didn't care about the politics of the Nazis. I had never voted for them, but I had followed their lure. Were we guilty? Was it my fault that British mothers had to mourn their sons?

I was overcome by darkness. The images of my fallen brothers came before me. Who was ultimately responsible for their deaths? We had invaded Russia. We had brought suffering to the world. Could I blame the enemy?

I closed my eyes for a moment and what had to happen happened. I fell asleep.

"They're coming!"

Someone pulled me up by the shoulders. It was the mute. "Fight!"

I was wide awake in an instant. I had lost my sense of time.

It could have been a few minutes or a few hours. There was already a lot of rumbling to the left and right of the front lines. Luckily we were spared from artillery fire this time. Still, goose bumps crept from the back of our necks to the tips of our toes. The earth shook. The roar of the engines grew louder. They were coming with tanks!

Ede ran through the positions. "Make your charges," he shouted to the men. "The British have crossed the Rapido. They've managed to get a foothold on our bank and have built two heavy bridges. Their tanks are advancing."

"Where's our Ari?" I countered.

"Bombed by the allied Jabos!"

We were lost. No Ari, no air force, and the enemy was attacking with tanks. The Gustav Line was crumbling.

Ede ran on. "Form small groups of three men! Let them roll over you and come from behind! It came over the radio. The Canadians were able to cross with a tank regiment."

Then he was gone.

The grenade launchers opened defensive fire while the Pak crews continued to lie in wait. They waited for the ideal distance for an effective hit.

Two more explosions went off in the former minefield. Each one stopped a tank but did not destroy it.

In the command posts, the radio coils were running hot. Transmission impulses were carried over the coils and crawled up the wires to the antennas. The radio transmissions were picked up by the receivers and voices croaked out of the loudspeakers.

Own detectors ran away and neighborhood detectors arrived. Strip-drawers searched for lines shattered by gunfire and shells to repair them. When the field telephones worked, officers barked to other officers that they needed reinforcements and called for artillery and air support. The reports came in thick and fast. The once insurmountable Gustav Line was behaving like a shattering pane of glass: first came the impact, then small cracks formed, which continued to burst, and finally the glass shattered into a thousand pieces.

I don't know which feeling was worse, lying in a barrage of enemy artillery or in a cover hole with a whole tank company rolling toward you. I made myself as small as I could.

"Old man!" I heard someone call my name. "Old man, come here!"

I lifted my head over the cover hole and recognized Hauptmann Schmitz and the mute. They both waved at me. They were crouching in a large crater near a rock. I hurriedly looked in the direction of the tanks. I could still make it. Without thinking twice, I grabbed my things, pulled my legs up and jumped out of the hole. I immediately lay down on the ground and crawled belly up to my comrades. The mute finally pulled me into her crater.

"It's safer here. You have to go around the rock here". Schmitz pointed to the bare, cold rock.

The humming increased rapidly, the earth vibrated. Armored howitzers crashed. Their shells exploded all around us. Our machine-gun nests began to fire. They were probably firing at the advancing infantry. That was a good thing, because if we really wanted to fight the tanks, we had to separate them from the accompanying soldiers.

As the first two Shermans roared past, my heart almost stopped. They were so powerful and seemed so impregnable. It was an unequal battle, steel hulks against men. The third tank rolled over my old cover hole with a chain. It sank in for a moment. The hole was more than half filled with dirt. The tank rolled on. If I had still been in the hole, I would have been in bad shape. I would have either died or suffered huge fractures and bruises. I was sick to my stomach. Schmitz looked over the edge of the crater. He was holding five hand grenades tied together in his right hand. The mute also had a concentrated charge in front of him. "Take cover!" he warned and slid into the middle of the large hole in the ground.

The next Canadian tank rolled past our crater, only about a meter away. We lay still, pressed against the wall, barely daring to breathe. While we were still inhaling the Sherman's exhaust and rocks and dirt were flying at us from the track, Schmitz jumped up and ran after the tank. He pulled the ripcord of the stick grenade and threw it at the rear of the Sherman while still running. The Landser immediately dropped to the ground.

"A crazy guy," I shouted to the mute.

He didn't hear me, but he too had crawled out of the crater. He waited for the explosion.

Boom!

Then he jumped up and ran after Schmitz. The giant pulled the ripcord and threw his load at the now standing Sherman.

Pow!

The blast enveloped the tank. You could only make out its contours. I saw my two buddies running back out of the haze. After the wind had dispersed the cloud of powdered smoke and torn the gray, billowing fabric, I noticed small flames flickering from the vents. The monster would soon be on fire. The crew disembarked. A race against time began for them. Life or a horrible death in the flames - only fractions of a second separated the two.

Shots rang out. Men screamed wildly. A machine gun rattled away. Buchecker and Schmitz reached the crater and slumped into it. Schmitz was pale. Panting and barely coherent, he said: „R…re…re…treat!"

I poked my head over the edge of the crater. Infantry were charging us. My rifle moved to the ready. I fired. Beside me, Buchecker and Schmitz also began firing.

"We have to get out! There are too many of them," Schmitz shouted, looking around desperately. "Up there! Towards the machine gun."

"Yes," Buchecker confirmed briefly and succinctly.

A new loading bar was inserted. When the bolt was pushed forward, the top round was fed into the chamber. Lowering the bolt handle tensioned the firing pin spring and locked the bolt. The carbine was ready to use again. "Go!"

Buchecker was the first to jump out of the funnel, but instead of moving quickly, he stopped dead in his tracks. He turned to me and narrowed his eyes.

"Ouch!" I heard from his lips.

His body jerked a few times. Dark spots spread over his back. My legionnaire friend's eyes were wide open. A thin streak of blood flowed from the corner of his mouth. He dropped the rifle, took two steps forward, and then toppled over like a felled tree.

"Nooooo!" I screamed desperately. I ran over to him and tried to pull him back into the grenade hole. "Come on, help me," I yelled at him. "Move!"

The mute didn't move. My hands grabbed his head. I lifted him up. His eyes stared into space. His gaze was broken. Buchecker was dead. Shocked, almost apathetic, I searched for his dog tags. I quickly found the silver chain and pulled on it. The dog tag slipped over his collar. I broke it off.

Schmitz grabbed my shoulder and pulled me out of my thoughts.

Rrrrt ... rrrrt

A barrage of machine-gun fire swept across the ground right beside me. Small fountains of dirt sprayed upward, marking the path of the fire.

"Come on!" Schmitz yelled.

Bang!

The Sherman was in flames. They had detonated the ammunition on board. The steel giant was literally lifted a bit and immediately crashed down again. The turret tilted sideways with an ugly grinding noise.

I followed Schmitz. We ran up the hill, crouched down, threw ourselves to the ground, looked around, got up and ran on. Ede and Krueger appeared in front of us. They waved at us. "Over here!"

The battle raged. Grenades whirled through the air. Tanks pushed forward. Infantry charged the positions and the enemy air force bombed. We lay in an inferno of fire, explosions and steel thunderstorms.

The company rallied. Within 500 yards, infantrymen followed the tanks as they advanced. Lieutenant Kohler himself was behind the radio, screaming into the ether for support. It was useless. All available forces were already engaged. To reassure us, we were told that the Canadian tanks had hit our assault guns and could be stopped.

Lieutenant Kohler ordered the men to rally and explained the order to be given. "Men, we are going to flank the British and cut them off from their supplies!"

I barely understood half the words the officer used to fire up the men. At some point I heard a loud "Hurraaaaa". We began to move as one. The machine guns had gone back to their positions and as we ran they fired a barrage.

Rrrrt ... rrrrt

The firepower of the MG 42 was feared. It was not without reason that this weapon was nicknamed "Hitler's Saw" and "Bone Saw".

The enemy was taken by surprise. Men fell to the ground, hit. Shots mixed with shouted orders. We advanced. Return fire came. Wounded men rolled in the dirt. Machine gun barrels glowed. Sometimes there was hand-to-hand combat. Men became animals. They fought to survive. They killed to not be killed. The machinery of war raged and there was no escaping it. I began to hate what I had once loved so much - the uniform.

May 19th, 1944

The last few days were unparalleled in deprivation and cruelty. In the end, we were only able to hold off the enemy for a few hours. The men fought like lions, pushed themselves beyond their limits, and still perished. The superiority was too great.

The battlefield was littered with smoldering wrecks and corpses. If you pushed a front, you pushed the enemy. We did, and so did the Allies. After a successful breakthrough, it was the sad task of the advancing troops to clear the battlefield. It could take days before the last body was found and recovered. When the sun shone, the process of decomposition accelerated. Bloated corpses were the result. These in turn gave off the sweet, unpleasant smell of decay.

The air smelled of exhaust fumes, gunpowder smoke, and death. A light wind drove this cloud of death over the land and enveloped it. In many shell craters, and even in some valleys, this stench, which sometimes smelled disgustingly like decomposition, hung in the air. You had to notice it, but you could never get used to it.

Most of our regiment and the entire division were already in the midst of fierce retreat battles. Again and again machine guns rattled or the dry fire of hidden Paks cracked. As darkness fell, we saw several blazing fires from our hill.

Our company strength was down to 20 men. We were huddled in our holes in the ground, not knowing which way was up, down, or behind. Everyone was exhausted. Our uniforms were dirty, wet, and bloody. The faces of the survivors reflected the indescribable horror of the front. We were spread out over a length of about 50 meters in funnels and holes dug into the mountain. Lieutenants Kohler and Ede conferred. They stared alternately at a map and through binoculars into the valley in front of us. Erwin lay behind his MG 42 and dozed. Krueger went from man to man. "Eat, my boy, and drink," he advised them all. "Now we have some rest to fortify ourselves. Leave the cigarettes out. As long as Tommy doesn't discover us, we'll have our peace!"

We were cut off. One of the young guys, I estimated him to be 18 or 19 at the most, was crouching in a hole barely ten feet from me, howling. He had removed his steel helmet. Only his neck and ears were cut off. His straw-blond hair was a little longer. It blew up and down in the wind, sometimes covering his forehead, then quickly tilting to one side, only to fall over his forehead again the next moment.

A slightly older companion crouched beside him, staring straight ahead in silence. Krueger snapped her out of her thoughts when he popped into her hole. He put on his best face and smiled. After telling them about eating, drinking and the smoking ban, he stroked their heads. At that moment, he was like a father to them. They obediently dug out their packs.

"That's good, boys. We'll get some food, then I'll take you back and you'll be home soon."

After that sentence, I recognized something like a smile on both of their faces.

I was probably largely responsible for my own fate. If I hadn't been so obsessed with uniforms, who knows where I would be now. Anywhere but probably not here, it flashed through my mind.

But these young men were robbed of their youth, their lives were taken from them, and they became instruments of evil.

I found myself thinking about this more and more. Was it the young comrades sent from home to the front to die, or was it the death of my brothers? Or whatever. It didn't matter. I hated the war and I hated the men and the regime that had imposed this war and all the suffering on us, the enemy and the world. How often did I have the Party bosses in my mind's eye. Countless times I pulled the trigger. Unfortunately not in reality.

Engine noise. We flinched. Erwin pulled the machine gun back into the pit where he was sitting. Four tanks had come up and stopped less than 100 meters from where we were sitting. We were sitting on the hill, they were probably not underneath for the night.

Krueger and Ede came to me almost at the same time. One wanted to ask me for food, the other wanted to get a better view of the tanks from my position.

The commanders stood in the towers and gave each other tactical signals. I pushed my rifle over the edge of the hole in the ground. Ede tapped me on the shoulder. "Don't!"

The barrel moved back. The engines shut down and the crews got out. The soldiers talked. Storm lighters lit their faces as some of them lit cigarettes. One walked off to the side and disappeared from sight.

"Stay down!" they whispered.

Silence for minutes. The Canadians' cigarettes were smoked. They ate in the last light of twilight. The commanders stood together, studying a map by the light of a flashlight.

"If we raised our arms and marched down there, the war would be over for us," Kruger breathed to me. He turned his head to the side and looked at the two young comrades.

"Forget it," Ede said harshly. "Lieutenant Kohler has contacted the battalion with the intelligence officer. We've been ordered to fight our way through. Anything else would be cowardice in the face of the enemy."

Kruger scratched the back of his head. "It was just a thought."

"A valid thought," I came to his aid.

"Orders are orders!"

We waited another two hours. The tanks remained alone. At least we didn't notice any infantry around. We figured that they would spend the night here and then move on the next morning. Lieutenant Kohler had taken stock of the weapons and ammunition at our disposal.

"Three clips for the carbine, two rounds for the rifle, 16 rounds for the 08 pistol," I reported.

The hope that we could make four or five concentrated charges of hand grenades was dashed. We had a total of seven hand grenades. Our company commander then made a decision. "This is enough to make it rumble down there, but no more."

"If we can get there, we can crack all four tanks," replied a sergeant I knew only by sight.

"You dare?"

A short silence. "If I can get five more good men to hold off the Canadians or take them out, yes!"

I cleared my throat. "One well-aimed shot and we'll have the whole lot of them on our backs. We're surrounded by allies, don't forget that."

"Afraid?" the sergeant asked with an almost expressionless look.

"Anyone who says he's not afraid is lying," I replied. "But that's not the question. Our orders are to retreat and rejoin the battalion."

The sergeant seemed a little irritated and was about to reply when Lieutenant Kohler spoke up: "Sergeant Schwarz, you lead the company back to the battalion. Sergeant Graf, you will form a squad of five men. We'll attack the tanks, try to blow up all four with hand grenades and then retreat. You," he looked at me, "... cover our retreat with the machine gun."

Tense silence. I was surprised that an officer spoke to us as if he were a simple soldier or sergeant. At that moment he was nothing more than a comrade, one of us. We were a bunch. We were the rest of the company. Tomorrow everything would be different, but today he was one of us.

Ede was the first to respond. "We have to go one, two, three or more kilometers through the enemy lines. Wouldn't it be better if we went together?"

Kohler replied in the negative. "The enemy is distracted when the tanks are burning, and I'm sure we'll catch up with you soon."

Sergeant Graf was emotionless. There are people you meet, don't know and don't like right away. He was the kind of comrade I would never have shared a beer or a glass of wine with. But he was also the kind of comrade I liked to have next to me in battle. He wasn't just uncomfortable with us, he was uncomfortable with the enemy. You didn't want to have people like that as enemies. So I thought it was good that he wore our field gray.

"We're going down. If we can surprise them and kill them quietly, we'll do it. As soon as there's a bang, we have to act quickly. We have to get the grenades into the tank with the safety off. Then we have about three seconds to get to safety."

Both groups were gone. The night had engulfed the bodies. I lay in my position, trying not to lose sight of the men. It was impossible.

About ten meters from me, Moonface and Roeder had positioned themselves with the machine gun. They were to fire a barrage as soon as Canadian or British infantry attacked or pursued our comrades as they retreated.

Minutes passed that seemed like hours. The whole situation was eerie. In the distance we could still hear rumbling at irregular intervals. The fires that had been burning had died down. Some of them could still be seen as glowing dots in the darkness. I concentrated on the tanks. I could faintly make out their outlines. Now and then I thought I could see a few figures scurrying around. But nothing I could shoot at.

Suddenly it started. It was shot after shot. Guns flashed. Men screaming. A loud bang followed, and for a moment there was a huge explosion. Flames threw a flickering light. Because of the detonation, I had my head down for a moment and pulled the rifle with the sensitive optics into the pit for protection. There was no impact from shrapnel, etc., so I immediately regained my position and brought the rifle to bear. It was still difficult to see targets. At one point, however, I was sure I could get a shot off. An armored soldier appeared in a turret. I had him in my sights long enough to fire and pulled the trigger. The shot rang out. There was a muzzle flash and I felt the butt of the rifle hit my shoulder from the recoil. The tanker was hit and toppled over. Two more explosions rang through the night. Another Canadian appeared in my Rifle scope could clearly identify him as the enemy by the bright glow of the fire. He was firing a machine gun. I pulled the trigger. The soldier fell to the ground.

A new clip had to be inserted. Practiced hand movements. Within seconds I had reloaded. When I looked through the sight again, the attack was over. Two tanks were burning. Men lay on the ground. I was missing a target. A short time later I heard them coming back through the darkness.

Erwin Mueller and Elmar Roeder grabbed the machine gun and the ammunition. "Get out of here!" they shouted at me.

Lieutenant Kohler and two men opened the door, but Corporal Graf was not there.

"Retreat!" shouted Lieutenant Kohler.

We walked through the night. The feeling of being followed was terrible. I felt like a child again when I had to fetch fresh coal for the oven from the cellar and felt the fear on my neck. I always thought a monster would grab me from behind and eat me. Covered with goose bumps, I would put the coal bucket down and was always glad to have escaped that imaginary monster. It felt the same now. And just like then, goose bumps spread all over my body.

The retreat went much better and easier than I had hoped. Except for one dicey situation where we missed a British unit by just a few meters, we made it through without any major problems and actually reached our battalion's rearguard, which had been left behind as security, at dawn. Ede and his comrades had arrived just ahead of us. They, too, had no contact with the enemy. The holes in the HKL created during the Allied breakthrough were only gradually being closed. That was our great luck.

Corporal Graf was less fortunate. He and two other soldiers had been killed or seriously wounded in the attack. Two of the four tanks were completely destroyed, while the tracks on one side of a third were definitely blown off.

I can no longer tell if we were being followed. We hadn't noticed any enemy infantry behind us.

The Gustav Line, which we had defended for six months,

had fallen. British units had bypassed Monte Cassino, Polish troops had stormed up the slopes. American and French units broke through the southern wing of the front.

Finally, our supreme commander, Field Marshal Kesselring, had no choice but to order a retreat and evacuate the monastery mountain. On May 18, 1944, the last German defenders of Monte Cassino raised the white flag.

Our regimental commander, Lieutenant Colonel Ziegler, was proud because the regiment was mentioned in the Wehrmacht report. The issue of the still existing sutler goods was welcome, but neither this nor the recognition of the OKW could replace our fallen comrades. The joy at the company level was correspondingly muted.

We had no peace. British troops advanced in the Liri Valley and took Pignataro. Canadian armored troops advanced with all their might towards Pontecorvo.

Regiments 200 and 361 of our 90th Panzer Grenadier Division gathered in this very section. The chaos was almost unbeatable, yet the formation and organization of the units worked. Strippers were laying telephone cables. Pioneers had hastily laid small minefields in advance. Pak crews had taken up positions with their guns. Tanks and assault guns had made themselves as battle-ready as possible, and the batteries of the 190th Artillery Regiment, which belonged to our division, were working feverishly to align their guns. Ammunition trucks rolled to the front, wounded transports to the rear. Wrecked trucks lined the roadsides.

May 24th, 1944

All able-bodied men were in the receiving positions at Pontecorvo. We resembled a ghost army and it was a miracle that the fighting spirit of the Landser seemed unbroken. Fighting spirit is probably the wrong word. It was more the will to survive.

None of us wanted to die.

Since yesterday, another fierce wave of attack has been rolling towards us. To the west, it crashed and raged like hell. The thunder of ship guns and artillery joined the bombs dropped by the enemy air force.

In addition to the clear material superiority, there was the mass of infantrymen storming behind the tanks against our positions. The battle could not have been more unequal, and yet we still lay in the trenches, behind sandbags, or nestled in the ruins of bombed-out houses, waiting for the enemy.

The engine noise of the approaching fighter bombers was deafening. First you thought you heard a swarm of bees buzzing, then the roar of heavy engines. Bombs were released and fell mercilessly on our positions.

Wham ... wham ... wham

Impact after impact was felt. The earth shook. Machine guns rattled again and again. A desperate attempt to get some of the planes out of the sky. Clouds of explosions showed the attempts of our artillery to break through the iron cloud and shoot down a few fighter-bombers.

Wham ... wham ... wham

They lay on the ground or cowered under some kind of cover, hoping to be spared. Most of the attack fell on the comrades of Regiment 200, for whom it was a pitch-black day.

As soon as the fighter bombers were gone, the earth began to shake again. This time under the weight of approaching armored vehicles. Their cannons cracked dry as they fired. The shells rumbled hard upon impact.

A group of tanks had gotten stuck in a minefield. We rejoiced as some of them were badly damaged and some were burning brightly. The columns of black smoke were directional signs for our weak artillery. A few shells hit, but the steel wall was not stopped.

The combat vehicles of the 5th Canadian Division rolled

towards our positions. Pioneers and a tank destroyer were in action as well as our assault guns.

Infantry followed. Machine gun fire flared up. Crouched in the ruins of a destroyed farmhouse, feeling well-protected, I fired one round after another. As a sniper, I was hard to spot in the ongoing battle. This saved me from having to constantly change positions, which in my opinion wouldn't have helped anyway, as the battle was raging all along the front.

The Canadians had almost broken through when Lieutenant Kohler's radio calls for help were heard. Assault guns caught the Canadians on the flank and forced them to fight. The tanks turned and duelled with the German steel tanks.

Meanwhile, strong Allied infantry units had continued to advance. Erwin emptied belt after belt with his MG 42. We were still able to hold off the Canadians, but the front was already dented in several places.

A dispatcher rushed up, threw himself for cover, panting and yelling: "The guys in the 200 have been overrun. We have to retreat. Melfa position!" His chest rose and fell like mad. His head glowed bright red. The signalman reached for his water bottle, opened it, and took a few big gulps. "We'll be leaving at nightfall, too," he added. He closed the bottle and ran off again. No sooner had he left the ruins than a bullet struck his helmet, piercing it and going through the detector's head. He fell like a felled tree and lay motionless.

Erwin raised the machine gun to his shoulder and pulled the trigger. The deadly weapon spat out its bullets. Casings flew away, the belt moved smoothly over the transport reel.

Rrrrt ... rrrrtt

The regiments of the 90th Infantry Division had been ordered to withdraw to the so-called Melfa position. The Melfa is a small river, about 40 km long, that flows into the Liri north of Pontecorvo. In some places its bed had dried up.

The withdrawal started around midnight. Together with the

MG 42 crew Erwin and Roeder I was supposed to form the rear-guard again, so we stayed in our position for the time being.

After more than half of the company had retreated from the front, the Canadians managed to break through with a shock troop. A fierce firefight ensued, but the enemy advance was cleared.

I didn't attach too much importance to it. Only after Erwin, Roeder and I had rejoined the company did we learn that Ede had been slightly wounded in the firefight and taken prisoner with three other comrades.

It was not over when they reached the Melfa position. The Allies followed with heavy vehicles. Again it was the Regiment 200 that rumbled the most. The enemy threatened to overrun them when help arrived from neighboring mountain troops. They pierced the enemy's flank, shot down more than 20 tanks, and helped the 200 retreat in an orderly fashion.

We also took prisoners. The two Canadians spoke only French and an interpreter was needed for the initial interrogation. I offered my services and was transferred with the two prisoners to the battalion command post.

The next day there were more heavy attacks and the division had to withdraw again. This time the objective was Arce. The village was about ten kilometers north of us on a hill. We took positions to the left and right of it.

The almost impregnable Gustav Line had fallen. Monte Cassino became the symbol of a battle between nations. 50 nations fought together against Germany to finally free Europe from the clutches of Nazi rule. We fought against an invincible superiority in men and material. We were under constant artillery fire and fought man to man. We were at the end of our tether and wanted only one thing: to survive.

Monte Cassino also became synonymous with hell itself.

Pain and suffering were felt on both sides every single day. Young men were sent into battle like lambs to the slaughter. We waded in blood and guts, we aged several years in a few hours and we suffered tortures that we would not inflict on our worst enemy.

Monte Cassino became the burial place of some 55,000 Allied and 20,000 German soldiers. Many of the men were barely 20 years old.

Their cries will never fade from the memories of many survivors on both sides.

June 1944

The battalion commander was impressed with my language skills and temporarily added me to his staff. I became the combat clerk's assistant, and from then on I was, so to speak, the Z.b.V. in the clerk's office. I was especially present during the first interrogations of prisoners of war. I also had to translate captured documents. As an additional task, because of my shooting skills, I was assigned to provide protection on various trips.

But this was not a quiet post. For the next four weeks we were moved from one focal point to the next. The completely exhausted 90th Panzer Grenadier Division had to plug countless holes and was constantly used as a fire brigade at the front. We were constantly on the move, and the combat strength of our unit had been drastically reduced. The logistical effort to move the entire division every few days was enormous. Advance detachments had to find suitable locations to provide shelter and food. Communications soldiers had to set up their communications networks and establish connections as quickly as possible, and the entire staff had to be disassembled and reassembled.

Trucks were unloaded. Equipment was hauled in, set up, and when you thought it was all done, the next order came to move on and clear the site. We hiked up the Italian boot in stages, and in the meantime were deployed in Tuscany.

The retreats were always fast, but at the end of June the ordered retreats were slow. The fighting troops were exposed to constant attacks, all carried out with heavy weapons. I feared for my comrades and found myself knocking on the boss's door several times to ask to be transferred back to the company.

Once there was a wonderful opportunity for conversation. The men in the typing pool had all gone to lunch at the same time, but the boss was still in his office. I went to the door to knock, but I hesitated. Images of my fallen comrades and the constant bombardment of enemy artillery raced through my mind. I clenched my hand into a fist, but instead of pounding on the door, I clenched it angrily. Just then the door opened and I was startled. The captain stood before me and looked at me. "What's the matter, old man?" he asked me. "You want to take me to dinner?"

"I... uh... no," I stammered sheepishly.

The officer looked at me. "Speak up. I don't have much time. We're moving again. If we stay any longer, we'll soon be in a cauldron."

More than once we were in danger of being surrounded by enemy troops. This time too. Another retreat was imminent. The enemy was pressing against the front. Memories came back. I simply lacked the courage to rejoin the fighting troops. I unclenched my fist and tapped my pockets with the palms of my hands in embarrassment. Then I took out my wallet and said: "Oh, there it is. I thought I'd left it here somewhere before. Have a nice meal, Captain."

"Meal, old man."

I left the office with the officer.

The very next day, trucks arrived and we loaded files, typewriters, and all sorts of other things. We were on our way back.

A stroke of fate hit us unexpectedly hard. Our regimental

commander, Lieutenant Colonel Ziegler, who had just been a-
warded the German Gold Cross on April 11, 1944, was killed on
June 25, 1944. We were all devastated. The lieutenant colonel
was a strict but good soldier who led the troops from the front.
He could often be found in the front ranks. This earned him the
utmost respect, right down to the rank and file grenadier. He was
shot in the head during a trip to the front near Prati in the Massa
region. His successor was Lieutenant Colonel Stollbrock.

I quickly got used to working in the typing pool again. This
time it wasn't the legion, but the battalion headquarters. My previous knowledge of interpreting and the art of typing almost
blindly and quickly proved to be a great advantage.

When I wasn't assigned other tasks, I used the time to read
the casualty lists. Each time I hoped not to find the names of my
comrades on them. So far I'd only had to read one familiar name.
Schmitz had fallen from my old group.

"The line is already very thin," I thought.

The shrill ring of the field telephone interrupted the typing.
The chief's aide was sitting with the artist over new maps. The
battle clerk stopped typing and took off the bakelite receiver. He
announced his unit, rank, and name as instructed. The caller seemed to take him by surprise. "Who ... what? There's no such
thing. Yes ... of course. Where is he now?"

He took notes and asked a few more questions before slam-
ming the phone down again. He looked at me with a big grin on
his face. "Altmann, do you know a sergeant named Eduard
Schwarz?" he said rather casually. "He was in your bunch."

I felt hot and cold. I knew that Lieutenant Köhler had just
written a letter to Ede's family. He said that since the last battles
near Cassino, Ede had been misplaced in the Pontecorvo area
and had probably been captured there.

"Ede? Of course I know him. He was my squad and platoon
leader. A good comrade. Why do you ask?"

The battle clerk laughed. "And he is one tough son of a

bitch. He escaped from a temporary British prison camp with three other comrades. They fought their way through the lines and got out with the paratroopers."

I couldn't believe it. There was a lump in my throat and I wanted to scream with joy. "Where is he now?"

The combat recorder glanced down at his notes. "They took him to the military hospital to have his wounds treated. Nothing serious, but open wounds are not to be trifled with. He developed a high fever in the hospital."

"His malaria again," I murmured.

"That's right. Malaria. Sergeant Schwarz is already on his way to the stage. They'll probably transfer him to a tropical hospital. Let him recover in peace." He stood and shook his head with a smile. "What a tough dog. Getting rid of Tommy in spite of his injury. I'll tell the old man right away. A division of that man's caliber and we'd still be in the Gustav line."

Ede is just a tough guy who never gives up, I noted in my diary. Underneath I wrote: "Some may have been there, but not here. Only those who have been on the front line in the drumfire know what hell feels like. Sometimes I can still hear them screaming.

That last sentence would haunt and shape me for the rest of my life.

July 2, 1944

A good four weeks after my involuntary promotion to stage clerk, I was still happy with my job.

"Some jobs you can't apply for, you're appointed to. And if you're offered such a job and you turn it down, you're screwed forever!" Heinz Krueger told me once when we were talking about typing pool soldiers and philosophizing about the best way to get there.

I was tired of fighting and killing, but I also missed my comrades Erwin Mueller, Elmar Roeder and Heinz Krueger. Along with Ede, I counted them among my best friends. And they were the only ones in my life whose fate meant something to me.

I also paid tribute to Lieutenant Kohler. He had given me the freedom to organize my duties as a sniper largely on my own, so that I could often be at the side of my comrades.

July was extremely hot and reminded me of Africa. The front was always a few kilometers away and only there when it was really noisy. Then I found myself flinching or trying to take cover.

My comrades had been fighting hard for days and were exhausted. I had a bad conscience about them.

The enemy had been attacking with massive armored forces for two days. More than 100 steel hulks rolled against the front and made several breaches. Only when all the tank units, tank destroyers and engineers were brought together was it possible to clear the danger spots.

Weakened and with heavy casualties, our division was again withdrawn from the front to be refreshed. The comrades of the 29th Panzer Grenadier Division freed us from the front line.

For us, the calm after the storm was the calm before the storm. In the Volterra area, the American troops prepared a major attack with heavy artillery strikes and carried it out with massive armored forces. Only the rallying of our artillery units prevented worse. The front collapsed again, but was still largely held.

By mid-July, the casualties in our units, especially among the officers, were so high that another retreat from the front was inevitable.

July 18th, 1944

The entire front was withdrawn to the Heinrich Line along the Arno River. The 90th Panzergrenadier Division had been bled dry and had put up a massive fight against the enemy until the very end. This was mentioned repeatedly in the Wehrmacht report. But what sounded like a heroic epic to some was in reality paid for with blood, pain, and suffering. Yesterday, many young boys marched beside us, happy and laughing; today, they lie dead in a mass grave.

We arrived near Florence and were refreshed by the remaining comrades of the 45th Regiment, which was about to be disbanded.

August 1944

The month of August saw coastal defense missions in Liguria and operations against partisans in the Alps. The latter had been equipped with weapons by the Allies. Under their leader Bruno Musolesi, known as "Il Lupo", the partisans had grown into an army of nearly 60,000 men. Among other things, they attacked our supplies and occupied important passes.

After one of these passes was taken by our regiment, our absence at the front was felt.

September 14th, 1944

We moved to the Adriatic Sea. There the 8th British Army attacked incessantly with heavy weapons and tanks. Our units were unable to prevent several breakthroughs and we had to play firefighter once again.

With the action at Rimini, my guest appearance in the writing room came to an end. Despite refresher training, there was a shortage of fit soldiers. My job in the battalion was assigned to a wounded comrade who had lost an eye and had voluntarily returned to the troops after his recovery.

Thanks to the contacts I had made during my time with the staff, I returned to my company with the best sniper equipment.

I can no longer say whether joy or sorrow took up more space. On the one hand, I was happy not to have been involved in combat for the past three months, but on the other hand, I enjoyed seeing my best friends again.

In the meantime, Lieutenant Kohler had been promoted to first lieutenant. Heinz Krueger led the platoon as sergeant and Erwin was still the machine gunner together with Elmar Roeder and a new young gunner.

The welcome was warm. Everything seemed to be the same as before. We sat in the back of an Opel Blitz and waited for Krueger. As always, he was almost late, jumped onto the back of the truck that was already pulling up, and grinned broadly as he showed off his organized treasures. I felt like I had come home.

"You've put on weight," Erwin said, his moon face glowing a deep red in the hot sun. His hair stuck to his forehead and beads of sweat ran down his sides. He wiped it with his sleeve and pointed up. "Damn heat. I didn't like it in Africa," he grumbled and laughed.

I rubbed my stomach and didn't think I'd gained any weight. "That's just your jealousy that I got to sleep in a real bed for three months."

"Children, look what Papa Krueger has brought," the organizer interrupted.

September 23rd, 1944

Everyday life at the front had once again taken hold of me. The dying around me were my daily companions, and the will to survive blocked every emotion.

The gates of hell had already rained down on us several times with a hail of shells from dozens of British guns and Ho-Witzers. Our artillery and smoke units responded with targeted fire, preventing several breakthroughs. A number of destroyed tanks testified to the ferocity of the fighting. Once again, the smell of gunpowder smoke and decay was omnipresent.

All the snipers of the battalion were in action. Our mission was to find and eliminate enemy Ari observers. We were also to eliminate as many officers as possible.

I was given enough cold food, packed three canteens of water, and sat on the side during a night attack near Poggio-Berni. Except for my equipment, nothing I had with me indicated that I was a sniper.

In the morning I had set up three well camouflaged positions between Poggio-Berni and Santarcangelo di Romagna. Gentle hills and small rows of trees and vines offered good opportunities.

Since our regimental commander had been shot in the head, I was convinced that there were also Allied snipers in the area. So I had to be doubly careful.

I only changed position once on the first day. It was dull and boring. Several times I wanted to give up, jump up and retreat. I lacked the patience and hunting instinct of a sniper. Nevertheless, I stayed where I was and observed everything around me.

The battle was raging and I was not far from it. It wasn't impossible that a stray grenade would blow me apart or that I would be found by an enemy shock troop.

I passed the time by watching insects, eating extremely slowly, or trying to remember and recite poems or song lyrics.

As darkness fell, I left the position and thought about where I would be more successful. I tried my third shelter. It was on a hill between a few cypress trees typical of the region. Next to it, the vines of a vineyard stretched along a small side road.

I had gathered enough greenery and laid it over my camouflage patterned canvas. Two sticks were used to hold the canvas up at the front. My field of vision was excellent. Even when a British reconnaissance plane made its rounds, I felt safe.

Again, the whole day went by and I noticed nothing. At night there was a rumble all along the front and I could tell by the trembling of the sky where the guns were being fired. Burning fires indicated the impact points.

On the third day I had just finished my morning toilet when I heard the sound of an engine. My heart was pounding as I watched the road with my binoculars. A scouting party appeared. Two open jeeps, each carrying four men, rolled down the dusty road. The senior soldier was a sergeant. Without thinking, I set my binoculars aside and raised my rifle. I took aim at the driver of the rear jeep, had him in my sights, and inhaled. Then I exhaled and held my breath. My index finger had long since reached the trigger point and only needed to be bent a little. I squeezed the trigger. Head shot. The man instantly collapsed. Panic was obvious. The jeep swayed. The passenger tried to grab the wheel. I unloaded and took aim at the front vehicle. The sergeant was in it. The driver stepped on the accelerator. I shot the British sergeant. Hit him in the upper body.

My mind was racing. Should I keep firing or run? My mind told me to retreat.

Contrary to my hopes, the second jeep had not crashed. It lay in the middle of the road. The driver lay dead over the steering wheel, the passengers had jumped out and were lying for cover. My rifle barrel moved back to the front vehicle. Two smoke grenades were fired at the enemy and I lost sight. Those were precious seconds for me as well. I immediately picked up the canvas, grabbed the rifle and crawled backwards on all fours. Screams reached me. Shots. First single shots from rifles, then volleys from machine guns. I heard more engine noises. One or more armored personnel carriers must have followed the two reconnaissance vehicles ahead. I hurried, darting between the vines and running as fast as I could. When I thought there was enough distance between me and any pursuers, I threw myself to the ground. I felt like a hunted animal. Fear spread through me. The sniper instructor's stories triggered horror scenarios in my mind. My nerves were on edge and I began to shake.

They're going to ram the barrel of the gun up my ass!

I got up and ran even faster. I was panting, my sides were burning. I couldn't take it anymore, so I threw myself to the ground and stayed there. My pulse was beating wildly, my head was pounding, and my sides were burning painfully with every breath. Sweat poured from my forehead. Dark patches of sweat formed under my armpits and on my back. I was thirsty. Unfortunately, I had hardly any water left in my canteens. I greedily took them and drank them down.

Suddenly an inferno broke out. Guns thundered and howitzers hurled their big calibers at our positions. The heaviest shells came from the naval artillery. Their shells left heavy damage or deep craters with each detonation.

Would the Tommy come by here? Should I hide my rifle and anything else that would identify me as a sniper? I immediately pushed the thought aside, because what if our own people found me during a counterattack? Unarmed? Would they consider me a defector and shoot me by law?

I was desperate. Since my first shot with the sniper rifle, I began to worry again. Who had I shot today? Was it really necessary? My hands began to shake. I buried my head in them and began to cry.

After the bombing and artillery fire, they came. Tanks and infantry. I had digested my little nervous breakdown, got my bearings, and wondered if I would even make it back to my own lines during the attack. I didn't think so. But what was I going to do? I decided to move towards our outposts and then make a new decision. I checked my rifle, pistol, and equipment. To be on the safe side, I put a fresh loading strip in the carbine. The pistol was loaded and there was a round in the barrel. I had packed a hand grenade and a smoke grenade. I took both out of the backpack and put them in the belt so I could grab them quickly if needed. Then I got up and walked across country to the next road. It was clear to me that it was impossible to reach my own lines during the attack. So I looked for a safe place to hide, threw my tent over me, and watched the road.

For a long time nothing happened. Only at dusk did a small convoy pass by. They were British ambulances. Infantry followed later. The night had become quiet. I took a chance and crawled out of my hiding place. My tongue was glued to the roof of my mouth with thirst. I sucked on pebbles to quench my thirst. I didn't care if I met friend or foe. The unspeakable thirst was terrible and I needed water. I packed up and set out. Contrary to all my fears, I actually made it directly to our outpost without coming into contact with the enemy. I made myself known early and was able to pass through.

I had to file a report that same night. Since the line wasn't working again, a dispatcher was sent to battalion headquarters with the information.

I also learned that the enemy had penetrated the front in several places.

September 27th, 1944

The Tommy attacked again. I had just gotten up and had a cup of spare coffee when the alarm went off. Cursing, I threw on my field blouse, grabbed my rifle and hurried forward. I didn't have the 08 pistol with me, nor my backpack with various equipment.

Men rushed around, orders were shouted. The earth shook under the impact of grenades. One of them must have exploded not far from me. I felt an enormous pressure and at the same time a sharp pain in my side. My body flew weightlessly through the air and I hit the ground hard. Then the memory fades.

I can't tell if it was the same day or the next. Men slapped my cheeks. I opened my eyes. Voices I couldn't understand reached my ears. I felt pain as I was lifted. Everything spun around and I fell again.

The next time I woke up, I was lying on a hard table. My uniform was torn. I tried to get up and was pushed back down. They were holding me down. Something hard and sharp was being ripped out of me. At least that's what it felt like. A small stream of blood followed. White rags, stitches in the skin. I groaned and collapsed again.

I didn't know how long I was in the hospital before I could think clearly again. I only knew that I was alive and that I still had all my limbs. I was relieved when I began to feel my body and was able to move all my fingers and toes.

British soldiers had found me and treated me. I had been hit by shrapnel and my head had been thrown against a stone. My fear of being recognized and mistreated as a sniper was quickly dispelled. I don't know if the fear was justified or not. There was nothing to indicate that I was a sniper, and I never mentioned it myself. I was just a normal soldier and was happy that my fears of mistreatment were not confirmed. On the contrary. The British treated me well. It was almost like being in Africa. People treated each other with respect.

During the first interrogation I gave my name, rank and unit. This matched my identity card and I was at peace. I hid my past as a Foreign Legionnaire from the British.

Fighter-bombers flew over me and unloaded their deadly cargo over our positions. I realized immediately that I was in the middle of a massive offensive. The enemy was moving against the front again.

After I had recovered to some extent, I was taken to Naples with other prisoners of war. From there we were taken by ship to Africa.

Again we were interrogated. This time French officers were present, looking for renegade foreign legionnaires.

After I had coped well with these interrogations, I passed through various POW camps in Algeria, Libya and Egypt. New arrivals kept us informed about the progress of the war and, finally, about the unconditional surrender.

The war was over, but our captivity was not. I had a lot of time to think while I was in captivity. I lay awake at night wondering if I was a criminal and a murderer. I thought about my comrades who had been killed and maimed, and I couldn't find an answer. I had to learn to live with the burden of war and cursed all military service.

Another year passed and my malaria returned. After more malaria attacks, I was one of the first POWs to be released. I returned to Germany in the fall of 1946.

Our family circus no longer existed. The death of my brothers and my time as a prisoner of war had taken a heavy toll on my parents. They sold everything and gave up the circus life forever.

I welcomed this decision. I was no longer bound to the family circus and was looking for my freedom in a city.

So I ended up in Ludwigshafen am Rhein with a few stops along the way. I was able to put my experience in the Foreign Legion and the Wehrmacht to good use. I started working as an interpreter for the occupying forces. Later, my office experience and language skills helped me get a good job in an office. I had finally found a new home.

And when the love of my life crossed my path one beautiful summer's day, I was as happy as I had been as a child for the first time. Hedwig and I had been married for over 40 years. We didn't have any children, but we were happy until the day she died.

My war experiences never really left me.

They always crept into my dreams. I would wake up at night, drenched in sweat, looking for cover from the approaching grenades, or with shaking hands because in my dream I was aiming at an enemy soldier and couldn't pull the trigger.

Likewise, some faces or experiences were so deeply etched in my memory that I was reminded of them again and again.

The post-war revelations about the unimaginable crimes of the Nazi regime cast a dark shadow over me once again.

I often wondered if we were blind then and how it could have happened.

I also wondered if I had burdened myself with a guilt from which no one could free me.

I have never found an answer to any of these questions.

All I can do is tell my story and warn against wars.

About 30 years after the battle of Monte Cassino, I met an Indian businessman in a hotel restaurant. We got to talking and spent the whole evening discussing various subjects. At some point we got to talking about the war and realized that we had been enemies during the fighting for the Gustav Line.

We were both caught up in our memories for a moment. Tears welled up in our eyes. We told each other about different experiences and how terrible that time was. Like me, the Indian war veteran had lost many of his friends at the front.

We paid respect to the former enemy and condemned wars. Then we remembered the many dead and wounded.

As we said goodbye, we hugged each other. It was like a belated greeting of peace. He said in English: "My friend, I don't know about you, but there were nights when I woke up and I could still hear them whimpering and calling for help."

I looked at him and replied: "And there are times when I can still hear them screaming."

The End

soldiers-grave-67510_1920

Glossery and Landser-Jargon (Landser-Slang)

MP 40 *also called "Schmeisser" because the name of the weapon's designer was applied to the magazines.*	Submachine gun 40, successor to the MP 38, standard submachine gun of the German Wehrmacht and Waffen-SS, bar magazine, 32 rounds, 9 mm Parabellum
PaK	Panzerabwehrkanone
MG 42 *Nickname among the enemy: "Hitler's saw"*	Universal machine gun model 42, (also year of introduction in the Wehrmacht/Waffen-SS), very effective weapon, caliber 7.92 x 57 mm
HKL (Hauptkampflinie)	Main battle line
OKW (Oberkommando der Wehrmacht)	High Command of the Wehrmacht
Gustav-Linie	Codename for a German defensive position in central Italy, about 100 km south of Rome, that ran right through the "boot". The fighting there became known as the Battle of Monte Cassino.
Scho-ka-kola	Caffeinated, round chocolate packaged in a tin can.
Sanka	Medical vehicles – signed with a red cross on white ground
Concentrated charge (original)	Prefabricated explosive in cuboid form, dimensions: 7.6 x 16.4 x 19.5 cm, weight with carrying ring: 3 kg explosive
Concentrated charge (several hand grenade warheads are bound around a stick grenade)	Emergency aid for blowing up obstacles, shelters or for defense against armored vehicles (the latter usually for blowing up chains or when attacking immobile vehicles)
z.b.V.	military abbreviation for: for special use

Eight-Eight	erman anti-aircraft gun (FlaK), caliber 88 mm, which could also be used for ground targets
Age	Nickname for: Superior officer (usually company, battalion or division commander)
Thunderbolt	Latrine / field toilet
Medic	paramedic
Goulash cannon	Field kitchen
"Sore throat"	Someone would like to receive an award (Knight's Cross, Iron Cross, etc.)
Dog tag	Identification tag (usually worn on a chain around the neck)
Chaindog	Military Police = Field gendarme, recognizable by the tin sign he wore
Suitcase (also heavy suitcase)	heavy grenade
Kübel o. Kübelwagen	Light, all-terrain military car (Volkswagen)
Kitchenbull	cook
Landser	German soldier's name (Landsknecht = mercenary fighting on foot 15th/16th century)
tinsel	Medal/als/also insignia of rank
Latrine slogan	rumor
Spieß (Spiess)	Company sergeant (usually a senior sergeant in the position of a sergeant major - he was recognizable by the two piston rings sewn onto his uniform sleeve)
String puller	Radio operator (soldier)
S-Mine	Abbreviation for shrapnel mine, fragmentation mine or spring mine. When triggered by a kick or tripwire, the body of the mine is propelled to

	about hip to shoulder height and explodes with a fragmentation effect. This weapon was so effective that it has found many imitators to this day.
Aunt Ju	A nickname for the Junkers Ju 52, a type of aircraft manufactured by Junkers Flugzeugwerk AG, Dessau. The most successful model was the three-engine Junkers Ju 52/3m from 1932, which evolved from the single-engine Ju 52/1m model.
Twelve-engined	Professional soldier (service period was at least 12 years)
TVPl	Military association place
UvD	Abbreviation for: Unteroffizier vom Dienst /Sergeant on duty (usually a special service to supervise the internal service, the UvD followed the instructions of the company sergeant (Spieß) and ensured compliance with military order at the end of the service. Among other things, he was responsible for waking up the soldiers, supervising the performance of cleaning duties and observing the night's rest)
WuG (weapon an equipment)	Weapons and equipment sergeant, usually a member of the combat team

Quick overview Ranks (not final):

US-Army / british Army vs. Wehrmacht

Crews and non-commissioned officers

Private E 1	Grenadier
Lance Corporal / Private First Class	Gefreiter
Corporal	Obergefreiter
Sergeant / NCO	Unteroffizier
Sergeant	Unterfeldwebel
First Sergeant	Feldwebel
Master Sergeant	Oberfeldwebel
Sergeant Major	Hauptfeldwebel *(Spieß)* *Stabsfeldwebel* *Sergeant Major (Spieß)* *Staff sergeant* *= not an actual rank but a service position*

Officers

2nd Lieutenant	Leutnant
1st Lieutenant	Oberleutnant
Captain	Hauptmann
Major	Major
Lieutenant Colonel	Oberstleutnant
Colonel	Oberst
Brigade General	Generalmajor
Major General	Generalleutnant
Lieutenant General	General
General	Generaloberst
Field Marshall	Generalfeldmarschall

More Books by W.T. Wallenda:

Now in English – the German bestseller:

The Sniper from Stalingrad

ISBN-13: 978-3759720580

188 pages, 9,99 €.

Stalingrad, 1942 - 19-year-old Alfred Miller, a member of the 100th Panzer Division, comes to know and hate the cruel horrors of war during the fierce and costly battles for the "Red October" factory. Thanks to his marksmanship, he becomes a sniper.

After the encirclement of the 6th Army, the young Austrian wanders through the ruins of the dying city on the Volga during the coldest winter in years, both hunter and hunted. Hunger, cold, misery, death and fear are his constant companions.

The war hits hard and merciless every day. The soldiers are brutalized, the hope of salvation dies. Ultimately, there are only two ways to escape suffering and a grim fate: either get on one of the planes out of the cauldron, or die.